VIOLINS AND VAMPIRES

VAMPIRES OF THE DAEMONVERSE #1

CEE BEE

COPYRIGHT

Newton, MA 02464
www.monsterhousebooks.com
ISBN 9781956114089

DEDICATION

For all those who kick ass, take names
and read books.

VIOLINS AND VAMPIRES

I hope you enjoy this revised and expanded version of my serialized book, Blood Slave.

ONE THOUSAND YEARS AGO

KING CAELIN

TWENTY-FIVE YEARS OLD

cotland, 1000 AD

Tonight, Clan MacGregor celebrates the Spring Equinox with feasting, music, and a contest called *Kill the Vampire King*. During this tournament, anyone may challenge me, King Caelin, to a wrestling match.

No rules.

No mercy.

All comers.

I fight on until death or morning. *Naked.*

Welcome to the best night of my year.

Many things happen before the contest begins. After dawn, I process through the castle complex with my queen and court. The afternoon features boat races along the coast. During the evening, my people enjoy feasting and music. Once night falls, everyone gathers at the sacred grove with its lone birch tree. The moon rises. The games commence.

Which brings me to the present moment.

Grinning, I stand on a muddy clearing beside our sacred birch. Moonbeams cast the rolling moors in an unearthly pattern of light and shadow. About a hundred onlookers stand in a circle, their bodies forming the round boundary line for the match. Once a wrestler is tossed into the crowd—or killed in combat—the fight is over.

So far, I've defeated twelve warriors. All remain alive. My current opponent is Tavish, a sturdy man with long red hair and a barrel chest. I'm tall and broad-shouldered with brown hair and blue eyes. As with every match, Tavish and I fight Roman-style. No clothing.

The crowd keeps up a steady chant. "Fight! Fight! Fight!"

Tavish and I slowly circle each other. "Mayhap this is a bad idea," he murmurs.

In truth, my opponent has reason to worry. I'm bloodkin, which means I'm born a vampire. By contrast, Tavish is nightling, so he's a human who was transformed into a vampire later in life. Compared to nightling, bloodkin are stronger, faster, and fear no sunlight. We also wield magic. In my case, I can control the will of others.

"You're casting spells," says Tavish. "Getting into my mind."

In truth, I do sense Tavish's pulse. I could easily tap into his life force and compel him to my will. I won't, though. There's no sport in it.

"Trust me," I state. "If I were in your head, you wouldn't be jabbering."

The crowd laughs. And not due to my teasing alone. While I'm coated in mud, Tavish's skin remains pale and clean. Instead of attacking, Tavish paces me. Every so often, he roars or shows his fangs.

We'll never finish the match this way.

I lunge forward. Tavish and I grapple. Our shoulders press. Each tries to shove the other down. Cool mud slides beneath our feet.

The crowd chants faster: "Fight! Fight! Fight!"

Tavish grunts with the effort. Angling my body, I kick out my opponent's legs from beneath him, toppling him into the mud. Fast as lightning, I clasp Tavish's right leg. In a shot put-style maneuver, I toss my opponent into the crowd. People step away from the potential impact point. Tavish slams onto an open stretch of green.

"The match is over," I declare. Stepping over to Tavish, I offer him my hand and help him stand up.

"I donna what went wrong," murmurs Tavish.

"Stop thinking about what *I* can do," I tell him. "Focus on your *own* attack."

"Easy words for you," counters Tavish. "You're bloodkin. I'm nightling and—"

"—your mouth is your hardest-working muscle," I finish.

The crowd laughs once more.

I set my hand on Tavish's shoulder. "We'll spar another time. I believe you can best me. We'll train on it, brother."

Tavish smiles. "Thank you, your Majesty."

I step back into the mud pit. "Who claims the next match?"

This time, a bloodkin steps forward. It's Breagha, a female warrior on my personal guard. Even before the match officially starts, Breagha leaps for me across the mud. Her arms and legs are spread out like a starfish.

In response, I flip onto my back, careful to ensure Breagha's belly hits my feet. With a vertical push from my legs, I launch her into the air. Breagha lands in a crouch on a bit of green that's beyond the crowd.

"The match is over," I declare.

Arching my back, I hop up onto my feet. Next thing I know, I stand before my queen, Elisava. All my manhood is close and fully exposed. Elisava blushes.

Ah, my sweet bride.

Together, my queen and I are a study in opposites. I'm burly with sun-darkened skin and brown hair. Elisava's pale and slight. The beautiful curve of her belly makes it clear that she's with child. My soul warms at the thought.

I wink. "Good evening, Milady. Are ye well?"

Elisava replies in her native Rus. "Da." *Yes.*

All the world fades away until it's only me and my queen. Suddenly, I want the night to be over so we can be alone. I scan the horizon line. *Not long now.* Direct sunlight won't hurt bloodkin, but it kills nightling. Once dawn arrives, the games must end.

I step back to the center of our makeshift ring. "Who challenges the king?"

A new bloodkin steps forward. This time, it's Hunter, my second in command… and the only other bloodkin who's as tall as I am. He has golden hair, green eyes, and a sharp wit.

"My turn," announces Hunter.

"I was wondering when you'd step in."

Behind me, Elisava coughs. All thoughts of the match vanish. Turning, I scan her carefully. Bands of anxiety tighten around my chest. Elisava's been coughing for weeks. There's no need for me to speak my concerns. My queen knows what I'm thinking. I pin her with a worried stare.

Are you and the bairn all right?

She nods and smiles. I know what she wishes to tell me, although she does not speak it aloud.

All is well.

Still, my protective instincts are on edge. It's a reflex to inspect the crowd for danger. I find the usual mix of vampires— both bloodkin and nightling—as well as humans. The men wear tunics and leathers, while the ladies are wrapped in simple dresses. The blood brothers and sisters stand aside in a group, all of them wearing their characteristic red cloaks. These are honored humans who serve as willing blood donors.

Some of the alarm and tension seeps from my shoulders. *There's no threat here to Elisava.*

"Why check the crowd?" Hunter gestures across himself. "I'm right here."

I chuckle. This is why Hunter makes a great second-in-command. The man has both wit and strength. Like Breagha, Hunter leaps for me without waiting for the match to officially start.

It's a sneaky move. *How I'll enjoy making him pay for it.*

Hunter and I grapple. Our muscles strain. Bodies twist. Voices groan. Long minutes pass while Hunter maneuvers me face-down into the mud.

"Ha!" cries Hunter. "At last, I win!"

"Not yet." I spring to stand. My momentum sends Hunter flying. In fact, he might have gone past the crowd—if he hadn't hit a particular obstacle.

I step over to Hunter. "You slammed into the sacred birch."

Hunter pats the trunk. "My apologies."

I offer him my hand. "Well fought."

"I'll get you next year."

With Hunter gone, I scan the crowd. "Who else wants a turn? The sun's about to rise. We've time for one more battle."

A female voice sounds behind me. "I wish to fight."

It's Iona, one of the clan's blood sisters. At one time, Iona was a squat woman with full curves and long black hair. Now, she's short and skeletal. Though only twenty years old, Iona's dark hair has all turned gray.

My heart sinks. If bloodkin feed from one brother or sister for too long, the human donor can lose their sanity. We have a name for it.

Red madness.

In the past, I always tracked all our blood brothers and sisters carefully. If any donor shows signs of illness, I make them live with other humans until they recover. But I've been so concerned with Elisava and our bairn, I've stopped checking on human donors.

Which means that if Iona's going mad, it's all my fault.

"Fight me," repeats Iona.

"Nae," I say simply.

"You canna stop me," counters Iona. "I have a right to battle. Your reign ruined me, just like you've destroy us all."

Hunter steps forward. "Quiet, Iona."

I shake my head. "Any in the clan may approach me. Perhaps Iona can fight with words and release her fury that way."

Hunter knows what I mean. There still may be time to save Iona. If she speaks out her rage, we could reason with her to get help.

Iona stalks closer. "Fyodor the Rus, a bloodkin raider, killed your father, the last MacGregor King. But when Fyodor's daughter appeared on our shores, asking for refuge? You didn't kill her. You married her. Fyodor came to reclaim his spawn. You didn't turn Elisava over. Instead, you killed Fyodor, bringing ill luck on us all." She points to Elisava. "Now, our queen is dying. She's diseased by the bloodkin plague."

Worry twists inside me. Everyone's heard of this plague and how it kills only bloodkin women. We've been checking vessels before they unpack their cargo. So far, none in the clan have fallen ill. I won't have Iona panicking the clan.

"That's enough," I say evenly. "We all can see that you're the sick one."

"Nae!" Iona tears at her red robe. The garment falls to the ground, revealing her naked form. A weight of sorrow settles into my bones. All Iona's veins are dark red, making her pale skin looks as if it's covered in a crimson web. It's the worst case of red madness that I've ever seen.

The crowd steps back. It's a wise move. Those with red madness can do anything.

"Fight me!" cries Iona.

"I've another offer." I extend my hand toward Iona. "Let's go to the Gray Woman. Perhaps she can heal you."

"You won't fight?" Iona's body vibrates with rage. "You leave me no choice."

And Iona charges toward Elisava.

Primal rage heats my veins. *This is my wife. My bairn.* I speed to Iona and set my palms on either side of her head. With one swift movement, I snap her neck.

Iona crumples at Elisava's feet, dead. Grief and rage battle it out inside me. *This is horrible.*

Rising, I check Elisava once more. A thin line of blood trickles from her ear. A jolt of alarm runs down my spine.

"Are you well?" I ask.

She forces another smile. "Of course."

"But, your ear."

Elisava wipes at her cheek. When she examines her fingers, bright blood glistens on her skin. "Ah. Tis nothing."

Despite my muddy body, I scoop Elisava into my arms. "I'll get you safely to bed."

"Please don't," says Elisava. "If I needed the Gray Woman, wouldn't I say as much?"

"Indulge me," I state. "While you're pregnant, I'll take no risks." I call to the crowd. "Allow a protective husband to end our night early." When I next speak, I force myself to appear calm.

"The festival is over."

～

Carrying Elisava, I rush up the hill toward the castle. My queen and I sleep in a chamber on the top floor. I gently set my wife in bed, then order the servants to bring her clean linens and broth. All the while, my thoughts darken.

Elisava's been coughing for too long. And now, she bleeds

from her ear. Iona may be right. This could be the bloodkin plague.

Hours slowly pass as I watch my bride sleep. I wash up, change, and try to convince myself that Elisava and the bairn will be fine. Eventually, I take a perch on the windowsill and watch the sea lap against the shoreline.

That's when I see it.

In the moonlight, a single Rus ship appears on the ocean. Our watchman's basso voice echoes through the night.

"Rus Ahoy! Rus Ahoy!"

Elisava awakens. "Rus raiders are here. Tis likely my brother, Konstantin. This is good."

I look out the window once more. Most of the Rus sailors keep to their vessel. One man marches through the shallows toward the castle. Although he wears battle leathers, this warrior doesn't carry any weapons.

"You're right," I tell Elisava. "This could be Konstantin. And it seems he's here to parlay."

Yet, even as I speak those words, there's no avoiding the truth: raiding ships bring trouble. Even if the Rus don't fight, then neighboring humans and nightling will see this as a chance to attack.

After pulling on my battle leathers, I grab my obelisk dagger —it's the best way to stake a vampire—and head for the door.

Time to meet the Rus.

KING CAELIN

*M*inutes later, I slog out into the surf. My warriors keep pace behind me. Off in the distance, the raider's boat still bobs about a half-league away. The lone Rus warrior marches closer. If this were Fyodor, I'd expect a trick.

But this is likely to be Konstantin. Elisava trusts her brother.

Even so, every muscle in my body stays alert. Long minutes pass. Concentric circles fan out over the water where the Rus approaches. The moon remains bright. And the wind seems to whisper, *Elisava*.

Angling my body, I inspect the landscape behind me. The castle sits atop its bluff by the beach. No light shines from the top floor. Elisava must be asleep. I recall her words from before.

If I needed the Gray Woman, wouldn't I say as much?

Sadly, Elisava is too headstrong for her own good. She wouldn't ask for the Gray Woman until it's too late. Which is why I asked Hunter to prepare my fastest horse and keep it by the castle gate. If things get worse for Elisava, I'm ready to act.

Over in the shallows, the man pauses a few yards away. He

wears heavy furs and his face is adorned with blue markings. His swagger and boxy frame remind me of Fyodor the Rus.

Must be Konstantin.

I raise my fist and issue a command to the warriors behind me. "Hold!"

My fighters stay in formation behind me as I wade out further. My senses heighten. Water gurgles as I move. The wind carries the scent of seaweed and salt. Moonlight glints on the shallows.

"Greetings, King Caelin," says Konstantin. His voice is low and rough. He tilts his head. This close, I can see echoes of Elisava—the siblings share the same high cheekbones and full mouth. A pang tightens my chest.

How is Elisava now?

I force myself to reply. "And to you, King Konstantin."

When Elisava's brother next speaks, his voice turns gentle. "I come with dark news. Have you heard of the bloodkin plague?"

My skin chills over. "Aye."

"Back in the Rus lands, all our bloodkin women are gone. The bloodkin plague killed them."

Numbness moves over my body. *What will this mean for my people?*

A darker thought strikes me. Konstantin isn't here because he cares for Clan MacGregor. Only one woman would make him take this journey.

"What does this mean for Elisava?" I ask.

Konstantin's mouth thins to a determined line. "I had the same question. To get an answer, I climbed Siniy Mountain, entered a sacred cave, and summoned Zhenshchina Vody. You know her as the Gray Woman."

"Aye, the Gray Woman is a water elemental," I state. "She can appear anywhere water flows. To summon her, we also visit one of her sacred caves not far from here."

"The Gray Woman told me Elisava is already ill, as are all your bloodkin ladies. I asked the Gray Woman to heal our people. She said that was too much to ask and vanished. I wouldn't leave the cave. Although I summoned the Gray Woman a hundred more times, she did not return. I came here to ask your help. Perhaps if you bring Elisava to the cave, then..." He leaves the logic out there.

"I understand. It is hard for anyone to refuse your sister." A sad smile rounds my mouth. "I'll take Elisava to the Gray Woman right away. Perhaps the cure for my queen will help all our ladies." The next question pains me to ask, but it must be done. "How long does Elisava have?"

Konstantin's face draws tight with pain. "The plague works slowly, then fast. The signs of the end are clear. When blood trickles from the ear or nose, they are close to death."

His words hit me like fists. "That has already begun." I start to slog back to the castle, then pause. "Do you want to see your sister? I'll grant you safe passage."

Konstantin lifts his chin. "Nyet. Elisava knows me too well. One look at my face, and she'll know she's done for. We all need hope." In the moonlight, it's clear how Konstantin's eyes shine with held-in tears. "I heard she's with child. Is that true?"

"Aye. And it's all the more reason for me to leave. Thank you for coming here with your warning. I hope there's enough time."

"As do I."

Leaving Konstantin, I head back toward the castle. My warriors watch me silently, waiting for orders I never give. As I expected, Hunter already has my horse by the gate. Once I set my bride atop our steed, it's a short ride to the Gray Woman's cave.

Please, let this work.

KING CAELIN

I ride through the night with Elisava on the saddle before me. As we gallop toward the Gray Woman's cave, Konstantin's words echo through my mind.

The plague goes slowly, then all at once.

Hours slog by. The sky lightens. Elisava falls into an uneasy sleep. At last, I spy the Gray Woman's cave. The entrance is a jagged break at the base of a cliff wall. I rush inside with Elisava in my arms. My heart beats with such fury, my pulse throbs in my temples.

The cave walls are covered in runes that have been deeply cut into the stone.

The Gray Woman heals and hides. Ask her for any boon, but be warned. Chaos lies ahead.

Cradling my wife in my arms, I stride deeper into the cave. A small stone shrine sits at the far wall. It shows a woman standing in a low bowl of water. I set Elisava onto the sand and speak the incantation my father taught me.

I summon thee, water of chaos, woman of light.

Strands of seaweed wiggle up from the cave floor. As the long cords rise higher, they twist into the shape of a human. At last, the green seaweed turns pale as it solidifies into the Gray Woman herself. She's tall, lithe, and wearing a silvery gown. Her ears angle upward. Just as her name promises, her skin's the color of storm clouds.

"Greetings, King Caelin."

I bow my head. "Gray Woman."

"Did you bring your army to threaten me?"

"Nae. It's only me and my bride. We're here about—"

"I know why you are here," interrupts the Gray Woman. "It was the same reason Konstantin bothered me." She looks down upon Elisava. "There is nothing I can do for her. I've tried with others. Even magic has limits when it comes to the bloodkin plague."

My heart cracks. "That can't be true."

Elisava sighs. "Don't despair, my love." Her voice is a hoarse whisper. "Now, you can find your fated mate. Your true wife awaits you."

"Nae, Elisava. I already have my fated mate." I pull her onto my lap. "Fated mates have marks on their throats. Only their soul's partner can see these glowing red symbols. You may think you don't have one for me, but I disagree." I kiss her throat gently. "Right there."

"Ah." The trace of a smile rounds Elisava's mouth.

"Fated mates also create unique magic between them," I add. "And we've made the greatest spell of all." I rest my hand on the slight curve of her belly. "Our bairn."

"Oh, Caelin." Elisava's eyes brim with tears. "I'm so sorry to leave."

My throat tightens with grief. "You'll always live in my heart."

"Promise me. Watch out for my brother."

"I give you my word."

Elisava stops breathing. *She's gone.* I hold her to my chest while tears stream down my cheeks. I've already lost so much. More will soon fade as well.

The women of my clan.

The future of my people.

My own will to live.

It's as if a great hole gets punched through my rib cage. All that was once worth fighting for seeps from my body. I'm no longer king. Who rules a nation of corpses?

I don't know how long I sit there. When I look up, the Gray Woman still stands nearby.

"I'm a water elemental," begins the Gray Woman. "You're bloodkin. Both of us are daemon kind. As such, we rely on magic to solve every problem. But humans are clever. They're forever creating little contraptions and storing up knowledge. One day, I believe humans will develop a power to rival ours."

My voice chokes with emotion. "I don't see how that helps my people."

"When that time comes, I shall combine human cleverness with my magic. Perhaps then I can save the bloodkin."

A chill runs through my veins. I cling onto the second part of her statement.

"What do you mean?"

"Konstantin was right to send you here. All the bloodkin women are doomed. Yet, that's easy to accept when none of them are dead at your feet. I've changed my mind. In honor of your wife and child, I shall revive your people one day."

Worry, grief, and joy battle it out inside me. If anyone can save the bloodkin, it's the Gray Woman.

"Thank you."

The Gray Woman transforms into water and vanishes. For my part, I hold onto my wife until her body goes as cold as my soul.

4

PRINCESS ALEXA

ELEVEN YEARS OLD

us Lands, 1000 AD

The snowy paths of Siniy Mountain are a maze that's built to
madden the mind and dull the senses.

How perfect. I do love a good puzzle.

I march through an old forest of evergreens. Ice hangs from
the pine needles. The rocky ground hides every footprint. All the
trees look identical. That's by design. Somewhere in these woods,
there's an entrance to an upper trail that winds to the mountain-
top. And there lies the cave of Zhenshchina Vody, the Gray
Woman.

My younger sister, Sash, trudges beside me. She's tiny with
golden hair and a nature to match. In terms of age, I'm pretty
sure Sash is eight while I'm eleven, although it's hard to know for
certain. We've been meandering the countryside for years. At
first, we were running from Norse kidnappers. Now, we search
out the Gray Woman.

Why seek Zhenshchina Vody? Sash and I are bloodkin. I fear

my sister is sick with the bloodkin plague. Once I find the Gray Woman, she'll heal my sister in no time.

Speaking of Sash, she marches along beside me, smiling while she tells one of her fairy tales. "My favorite story is Queen Belobog and King Chernobog," says Sash. "Once upon a time, they were a regular human king and queen. She was all things light and sunshine, he was darkness and death."

While Sash rattles on, I pull out the pendant I stole from a Saxon nightling. It looks like a wooden disc that's covered with the carving of an intricate triangle. In reality, it's a map to finding the Gray Woman atop Siniy Mountain. I run my finger across the pattern and contemplate our next turn.

"But then, everything changes," continues Sash. "Belobog and Chernobog see marks on each other's necks—the image of an entwined sun and moon. They fall in love and magic transforms them into the first bloodkin vampires. That makes Belobog and Chernobog the original fated mates of our people."

"That's fine, Sash."

"Fated mates are rare along bloodkin, but I think you and I have them."

"Sure."

Sash is so sweet. She belongs back in the palace with my step-mother, reading stories and playing with dolls. I don't have the heart to tell her that the tale of Belobog and Chernobog isn't true.

Memories appear. I picture the onion dome of our palace as it crackles with fire against the night sky. Servants' bodies blaze as they jump from the windows. I weep while dragging Sash across a smoke-covered field. Shivers move up my spine.

Focus, Lexa. Leave the palace behind. You must help Sash.

Shaking my head, I force myself to refocus on the moment. "Where's Anya?" She's an adult human that I talked into helping us. Sash and I look more believable—and less easy to attack—with a grown up along.

Plus, everyone wants to kidnap vampire royalty. Anya's a

human. She helps hide the fact that Sash and I are bloodkin.

Anya steps out from behind a tree. "Do you see this?" Anya's tall and lovely with dark hair and pale skin. Like always, she's wrapped in heavy furs and scarves. Anya extends her hand to show some kind of yellow sap. It's yet another treasure for her collection.

I half-listen as Anya explains where she found the sap and how she can use it in a poultice. It's hard to seem very interested. None of Anya's creations cure the bloodkin plague. That said, I'm glad she has something to keep herself busy. Following me and Sash around can't be too enjoyable.

With Anya back, I lead us through the forest and into a snow-covered clearing. There's a break in the trees on the opposite side. My heart soars.

"It's here," I declare. "If we go through those trees, we'll find a path up the mountain."

Sash scans the mountain itself. "That's really high." I know what she means. The path itself will be a thin one. Even worse, a rock wall will border us on the left... and nothing but a deadly fall will be on the right.

I pat my sister's hand. "It's fine, Sash. I'll be behind you."

Rustling sounds nearby. I step about in a slow circle. All my senses are on high alert. The barest smell of vinegar and garlic fills the air. That means humans are nearby.

"There are others in the forest," I announce. "We better hurry."

"I smell them, too," says Sash. "I bet they want to see the Gray Woman, same as we do." She coughs. A light spray of pink settles onto the snow. My eyes widen. Now, there's blood in Sash's coughs. My sister is getting worse.

Anya notices the blood as well. "We better get hiking if we're to reach the Gray Woman's cave before sundown."

I wrap my arm around Sash's shoulder and lead her toward the icy path.

Not long now.

5

PRINCESS ALEXA

The three of us march slowly up the mountain trail. More than once, we almost slip off. Wind whips through our clothes and tears at our skin. Still, we're somehow able to reach the summit.

At last, Sash, Anya, and I step inside the Gray Woman's cave. It's a small space. A spray of snow covers the stone floor. By the far wall, there sits a small pedestal that holds the carving of a woman.

"What do we do now?" whispers Anya.

"Remember the spell I bartered off that Norse hedge witch?" I ask.

"Da," says Sash at the same time Anya says, "Nyet."

"Follow me." I kneel before the shrine and speak the incantation.

I summon thee, water of chaos, woman of light.

The air turns so heavy, it seems to press in around us. Seaweed winds up from the center of the cave floor and into a humanoid shape.

My body turns numb with awe. *This is really happening.*

Before us, the green weeds turn gray before solidifying into the shape of a beautiful woman with pointed ears. She reminds me of the dancers who used to come to our palace, only she's the color of pale charcoal. All of a sudden, it's hard to pull in a breath.

We're here. This is real.

The Gray Woman slinks closer. Sash grabs my hand.

"How did you three get here?" asks the Gray Woman.

"I was the one who found you," I reply. "We're here to heal my sister, Sash. Anya came along because she wanted to meet you."

"You think your sister has the bloodkin plague," states the Gray Woman.

"Yes," I reply.

"First things first." Lifting her arm, the Gray Woman pulls down the furs covering Anya's neck. Since it's winter, I hadn't wondered why Anya never removed her furs in front of us. Now, I see the truth. For the first time, I can make out bite-mark scars along Anya's throat.

She must have been a blood sister.

"Tell me." The Gray Woman lowers her hand, allowing the furs to recover Anya's scars. "How did you avoid the red madness?"

"Make me your apprentice," retorts Anya. "And I'll tell you."

"No," I declare. "The three of us have an arrangement. First, we heal Sash. Then, Anya can ask for whatever she wants. Each of us should get one wish." I refocus on the Gray Woman. "My sister is sick. Sash's wish must come first. Will you please help her?"

The Gray Woman looks between each of us in turn. "I'll grant a wish... but only for one of you."

"That's easy," I state. "Help Sash."

"That's your request, not my decision. I grant the wish to Anya."

My mouth falls open with shock. "That's not fair."

"I'm a water elemental. That makes me chaos, not justice." The Gray Woman looks to Anya. "What do you wish?"

"But each of us should get one," says Anya.

"Now, there's only you." The Gray Woman narrows her eyes. "Ask."

My heart pounds. Anya has no real loyalty to me or Sash. We can't have come so far just to have my sister die.

Long moments pass. At last, Anya speaks. "This is my wish. I want safety and freedom for me, Sash, and Lexa."

The Gray Woman purses her lips. "That's impossible. The young one is sick with the bloodkin plague. I cannot cure it."

My knees go wobbly. *She can't help Sash?*

"They aren't *full* bloodkin," explains Anya. "Neither have their fangs yet. I've heard the stories. If they aren't full vampires, then you can use your elemental magic to turn them into humans. That way, Sash and Lexa will be safe from the plague."

My heart warms. Anya really cares for us. I'd lost all my family in that fire. I didn't realize how important Anya had become to me.

"And what will happen to these two newly-human girls?" asks the Gray Woman.

"I will care for them as my own." Anya sets her right hand on my shoulder. At the same time, she rests her left palm against the back of Sash's head. The movement is protective and wonderful.

All this time, I'd thought of Anya as a mercenary. But when the time comes to decide between her wish and ours, she choses us.

The Gray Woman turns to me. "What do you say, Princess? Suppose I make your sister a human?"

"If Sash becomes human, that's what I want to be."

"And I believe you," says the Gray Woman. She inspects me and Sash carefully. "Have they tasted blood?"

"No," replies Anya. "Only human food."

"Then indeed, I could turn them into humans," says the Gray Woman.

Anya exhales. "Thank you."

"Only, I haven't promised to do anything," counters the Gray Woman. "Are you girls familiar with the idea of fated mates?"

"I know all about it!" cries Sash. "There's the story of Queen Belobog and King Chernobog. They saw marks on each other's necks and became the first bloodkin. Then, they formed our people and lived happily ever after."

Poor Sash. She really clings to her fairy tales.

"That's one of my favorite stories as well," says the Gray Woman. "Which is why you two shall remain bloodkin."

"What? You won't turn them into humans?" asks Anya. "That wasn't my wish! You see what the bloodkin did to me. They don't deserve to exist."

A chill runs across my skin. Anya claimed to be traveling with us because she wanted to meet the Gray Woman. Now, I wonder. Is Anya here because Sash and I are bloodkin?

The Gray Woman sniffs. "You don't come into my cave and make demands. Besides, I don't wish the bloodkin to die out."

"Yet, I do." Anya points to her neck. "You see how they treated me."

I recall the layers of scars and wince. I always thought blood sisters were happy and safe. How could this happen?

"I've a soft spot for bloodkin," says the Gray Woman. "Humans come and go like gnats, buzzing in and out of my caves. Bloodkin live long enough to make an impression. It's extremely rare for bloodkin fated mates to find each other. But when they do, each couple brings new magic into this world. It was the third set of fated mates who gave their people the power to make nightlings, did you know that?"

Everyone knows how bloodkin make nightlings. We drain a human's blood and then feed them our own. I didn't realize there was a fated mates story behind it all, though. Sash looks thrilled.

"All bloodkin are a pestilence," counters Anya. "Once we get rid of them, the nightling will die out as well. And this moment, right now, we can end them. Won't you make the girls human?"

"No," says the Gray Woman slowly. "Still, I shall grant your wish in my own way."

The Gray Woman crooks her finger at me and Sash. We both step closer. "I won't turn you human, but I will protect you. I'll take your memories… freeze your bodies… and while you're on ice, so to speak, I'll seek a cure for this plague."

My head feels loose on my shoulders. "So you *can* save Sash?"

"It's humanity that will save her," corrects the Gray Woman. "They're constantly tinkering with the physical world because they can't touch the magical one. When the time is right, I'll defrost and release you. From there, it's your choice what to do."

"That is *not* my wish," counters Anya. "I told you, I want them to become human."

The Gray Woman shrugs. "There's what you want. And then, there's what I'll do. You asked to watch over these two as a mother. I'll grant that part of your wish."

All of a sudden, new lines of seaweed erupt from the ground and wind across the floor. The long strands encircle Anya and Sash from head to toe. The cords whirl around me as well. It's so cold, my teeth chatter.

The Gray Woman leans over me. "One piece of advice. If you meet someone you're drawn to, stay close. Interesting things may happen."

I try to listen, but I can't focus on her words. I'm too busy trying to break free. Anya and Sash are already encircled in seaweed. Now, the cave floor glistens like liquid silver instead of rock. The seaweed drags both Anya and Sash into the ground.

I keep fighting.

Two new figures step into the cave. These must be the strangers I heard in the forest—the ones we thought were seeking out the Gray Woman. They've found her, the same as we have.

The Gray Woman turns to the cloaked figures. "A brother and sister have come to visit me. What might your names be?"

Even though I'm fighting icy weeds, I can still tell one thing. The Gray Woman knows exactly who these two are.

The girl speaks first. Although she's wrapped in furs, I can tell her face is covered in blue tattoos. She's also a lot older than I am. "We wish to be called Prudence and Viceroy."

"Not Viceroy," corrects the boy. "I'm Vice." He's Sash's age with a pointed chin and greedy eyes.

"We changed our names," says Prudence. "We're actually Rus."

"You don't say," intones the Gray Woman. "What clever disguises. I've been expecting you. You've here to avenge... who is it again? King Konstantin?"

"No!" cries Vice. "We're loyal to Konstantin's father, Fyodor the Rus. We were the only unbitten humans in his court. Fyodor trusted us to find new blood slaves for him to drain."

"Fyodor's son is now on the throne," adds Prudence. "King Konstantin is weak. He only takes willing human donors."

"I see." The Gray Woman smirks. "You two ran a blood slave gang, trapping humans as feeders. I shouldn't help you at all. You're only complaining because you no longer get gold for innocent blood."

Prudence scowls. "We must avenge King Fyodor!"

"Quiet yourself," says the Gray Woman.

Vice raises his fist. "You must—"

He never finishes. The Gray Woman lifts her arm. Lines of seaweed whip out from the cave walls, holding Vice and Prudence in place. Even more loops cover their mouths.

"How I loathe human whining," says the Gray Woman. "As it happens, your little mission fits quite well with one of mine. Much as it disgusts me, I'll help you."

As with Anya and Sash, the seaweed wraps about Vice and Prudence, pulling them into the now-liquid cave floor.

And I keep fighting.

Little by little, the Gray Woman turns toward me. "Are you still pushing back on my magic?" She lets out a low whistle. "Lots of strength in you."

The Gray Woman waves her arm. Icy seaweed covers my head. As the world goes dark, the Gray Woman speaks again.

"Don't worry, little bloodkin. I'll defrost you in a thousand years. Of course, you won't remember any of this happened, but you'll still be alive."

A thousand years later, Lexa is eighteen years old, living in New Jersey, and has no memory of her past.

6

LEXA

EIGHTEEN YEARS OLD

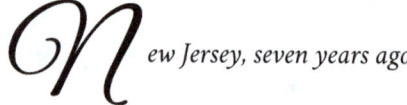 ew Jersey, seven years ago

I stand before a metal door that reads, *James Brookhollow, School Counsellor, Paxton High School, New Jersey.* It might as well say, *Lexa's Personal Hell.*

I knock on the door and count to three.

No answer.

Oh, well. Guess he's not here.

That works for me. I'd rather hit gym class than talk to Mr. Brookhollow again. I'm two steps away when a cheery voice echoes through the closed door.

"Come on in, Lexa."

My shoulders slump. *Crud.*

I step into a small office that's crammed with old books and new piles of paper. Motivational posters cover the walls, saying things like, *You can do it!* and *Leaders made here.* Behind a cramped wooden desk there sits a baby-faced guy with twinkly eyes, dark skin, and a corduroy suit. Mr. Brookhollow.

"Nice to see you, Lexa."

I slump onto the chair across from his desk. "Hey."

"Let's get back to it," says Mr. Brookhollow. "Are you still having hallucinations?" He clears his throat. "I mean, visions?"

"You can call them hallucinations."

Because that's what they are. Unfortunately, I recently had an hallucination in Chemistry class where I started yelling about a Gray Woman at top volume. That's what landed me in here.

"Just close your eyes and tell me what you see," says Mr. Brookhollow. "This is a safe space. There will be no judgment."

"Are you sure that'll help?"

"The sooner you talk about your visions, the better."

I stifle a groan. "Okay. I had one last night. One second, I'm watching a movie on my laptop. The next thing I know, I'm in this cave with a pale woman. For some reason, I'm getting wrapped up in seaweed. Everything is dark for what feels like forever. Then, a mystery person calls my name."

As I keep describing my hallucination to Mr. Brookhollow, my mind makes me relive it all over again.

A voice awakens me. "Get up, Lexa."

Opening my eyes, I find myself laying on a silver table in a white room. Sash rests on the table beside mine. Anya stands nearby.

"Look," says Anya. "She's awake. Hello, sleepy head."

I sit up. This can't be right. I was just in a cave. Now, I'm in an all-white room for some reason. Even more strange, I wear a thin tunic that opens down my back.

"What's going on?" I ask. "Where's the Gray Woman?"

"You're Alexa Uznetsov and you're eleven years old," says Anya. She stands beside a strange man with cropped black hair and blue marks on his face. No doubt about it—that man is Rus.

But, if Anya and the Rus both seem somewhat familiar, the way they dress is completely new. The two wear cloth pants and strange shirts. Anya has a scarf around her neck. The fact that Anya's covering her throat seems important, only I can't remember why.

"What is this place?" I ask.

"You're in the hospital," says Anya.

I scan the room. The chamber is all white. "I've never seen anything like this before. What's a hospital?" I slide off the table to stand.

Sash wakes up. She slips off her own table and comes over to my side. "Lexa, what's happening?"

"We're in a hospital," I reply. "Anya was about to explain what that means."

"A hospital is a place of healing," says Anya.

"Isn't that what the Gray Woman's cave is for?" asks Sash. "She's the healer. How did we get here?"

Anya sighs. "There is no cave. You two have always lived with me and your father. There was a terrible fire. Our home in California burned to the ground. The pair of you inhaled so much smoke, we thought you might die."

I nod slowly. There was something about a fire. I lived through it, same as Sash. Only, I can't grasp any details. "Why don't I remember?"

A look flashes across Anya's face. It could be guilt, but the expression is gone too quickly to be sure. "You've both been in comas for weeks," says Anya. "It's been so traumatic, the two of you lost your memory."

I frown. The Gray Woman said something about taking away memories, only I can't recall any details. Although I can't summon up the specifics of my past, I do know one thing about the present moment. Anya isn't telling the truth.

"I don't understand, Anya," I say. "Since when did we ever have a home?"

"Don't call me Anya. I'm your mother."

I focus on the man. "And who are you?"

"Your father, Mikhail."

Sash curls up against me. "We were in a cave. It was cold."

Anya leans over so she can look at Sash, eye to eye. "That's all right, honey. The doctors said you'd create an alternative reality. Your mental shock was so severe, you'll need to relearn everything about this world. Still, I've good news for you. We've moved to New Jersey."

I do a double-take. "What's a New Jersey?"

This time, Mikhail answers. "Even though your comas are over, your sister is still sick. We can treat her symptoms here."

I nod slowly. "Sash is sick, that's right. It's a plague." I press my palm against my forehead. "I can almost place the name."

"It is NOT a plague," says Anya. "Sash is sick with a rare kind of blood poisoning." Anya looks to Sash. "You inhaled a strange mix of chemicals during the fire. The only place that can heal you is a company called Silver Pharma run by the famous Dr. Gray. The place is based in New York, but we can get your treatments here."

There was a lot of nonsense in that statement. Before I have a chance to process it all, Mikhail speaks again.

"I work for someone named Konstantin King."

Sash pipes up. "I remember him. He's a Rus vampire."

Anya pinches Sash's cheek. "He's a businessman, honey. And Dr. Gray from Silver Pharma insists that Mikhail must work for Konstantin. It's the only way she'll supply the meds that Sash needs." Anya raises her hand, showing off a small shiny tube. "This is a plasma pen. If Sash injects one of these every day, then her symptoms will stay under control."

Mikhail beams. "Konstantin is a good friend of Doctor Gray."

I pinch the bridge of my nose. "This is making my head hurt."

"Where are the vampires?" asks Sash. "What happened to the bloodkin?"

"Please, don't talk nonsense," says Mikhail. "There's no such thing as vampires. It's all just ancient stories."

"You're lying," I announce. "Bloodkin are real."

"You just need time," says Anya smoothly. "And once you relearn the world around you, you'll accept it and us. Don't you want to start your new life?"

I pull Sash closer and consider. I don't remember much, but there was certainly a fire. And something deep inside me does trust Anya. She wouldn't press me and Sash into anything dangerous. I force myself to reply.

"Yes, Mom. I do want to start over."

"Good." Mom beams. "You may not believe this now, but one day, you'll hate the very mention of vampires. Your father and I will make sure of it."

I blink three times, clearing my mind. The real world reappears. Sure enough, I'm back in Mr. Brookhollow's office. "Did I say all that out loud?"

Mr. Brookhollow nods. "You did."

I hug my elbows. "I know it's another hallucination. I can't stop them."

"Look," counters Mr. Brookhollow. "Your home in California burned down while you and your sister were very young. Your mind is creating an alternate reality where you were placed on ice and revived. It's a coping skill."

"Doesn't feel that way."

"Please, try not to look upon it as something bad," urges Mr. Brookhollow. "Your mind wants to protect you from something you aren't ready to process. But if we keep talking, I think you'll work it out."

The bell rings. School is over. I stand. "Better go. Don't want to miss the bus."

"See you next week, Lexa."

"Sure. Thanks, Mr. Brookhollow."

Some small part of me says that my current reality is the lie, not my visions of the Gray Woman. But I push those thoughts aside. I need to get better. Believing in nonsense won't help.

After all, Mom is right. There's no such thing as the Gray Woman, let alone vampires.

7

LEXA

$\mathcal{M}$inutes later, I'm riding the school bus home with Sash. It's your standard crayon-yellow deal with gray bench seats that are arched on the top. You know, like tombstones.

Sash sits beside me. We tried for a spot at the back of the bus, but only scored something halfway down. I wear gray sweats with a boxy Paxton High T-shirt. Sash is in a yellow sundress that matches her bright attitude.

"Did you ever hear the story about Sister Alionushka and Brother Ivanushka? It's like Hansel and Gretel, only there's a goat involved."

While Sash tells the story for the umpteenth time, I scheme about ways of convincing Mom to let me drive to school. It's not like we don't have enough cars back home. And riding the bus is a pain.

My sister elbows me, snapping me out of my thoughts. "Were you listening to me?"

"Not closely."

"I know what you're really thinking about."

Which she does, because that's Sash. Still, it doesn't hurt to check. "And what is that?"

"You're scheming about how to drive us to school," replies Sash.

Busted.

"There's no point," continues Sash. "You know how Mom is about fitting in." Sash does her Mom impression, which involves talking in a high-pitched, sing-song voice. *"Regular modern children take the bus to school."*

Mom's really big on what *regular modern people* do. I've tried to explain to her how no one uses the phrase, *regular modern people.* It's one of the many odd things about Mom being Mom, along with the constant neckerchiefs she wears. I swear, there are flight attendants with way fewer throat scarves than Mom has. She even wears one that matches her nightgown.

A memory knocks at the back of my head. Mom's hiding something about her neck. As soon as the thought hits me, I push it aside. I have a long list of things I want from Mom. Being able to drive to school is far more important than the whole *take off your neckerchief once in a while* thing.

"You've gotten really good at Mom impressions," I say.

Sash grins again because, that's Sash. "Thanks."

One of the *comrade kids* comes over--that's what we call other students whose parents work for Konstantin. His name is Igor and he's a computer wiz. Which makes sense, considering how Igor's parents are in the *black hat hacker* part of Konstantin's mob.

Igor pauses by our bench seat. The guy has a square jawline, bright blue eyes and a swimmer's build. Honestly, he's single-handedly doing great things for the name Igor.

Nice as Igor is, all conversations with my classmates suck, hard. Eventually, the chatter comes around to asking if I'm still seeing the Gray Woman instead of Chemistry class. In situations like this one, I rely on a trick Mom taught us; it's what to do whenever someone sketchy is nearby (which to Mom means either Konstantin or a possible FBI agent.) I must repeat the mantra in my head.

Act submissive.
Don't make eye contact.
Be invisible.

Which I do. This time, I especially lean into the last phrase.

I'm invisible. I'm invisible. I'm invisible.

Meanwhile, Igor and Sash gab about some party this weekend. Although my sister's only a Freshman, all the Seniors want her at the fest. Not that I blame them. Sash flits around any room, smiling and making small talk with everyone. She's the perfect guest.

Me? Not so much.

Sash elbows me. "You remember Igor, don't you?"

I stop my inner mantra. "Sure."

But then, I pick it right back up again. *I'm invisible. I'm invisible. I'm invisible.*

"Right, um…" Igor snaps his fingers at me. "What's your name again?"

"Lexa," says Sash. "She's my sister. Remember, we all used to play Legend of Zelda in the basement?"

Igor smiles. "Oh, yeah. I remember that. Sash, you are a gaming monster!"

My sister blushes. "Thanks."

Igor frowns. "And you were there, too?"

"Excuse me," I tell Igor. "I need to write in my notebook now."

Which is also true.

At this very moment, the bus is driving past the headquarters of St. Peter's Shipping. It's one of Konstantin's front companies for moving ill-gotten cash. I make note of what trucks are on the loading dock and which cars sit in the employee parking lot. When I'm finished, I notice Sash is giving me one of her *'I'm not as happy as I could be'* smiles. Igor is gone.

I look up. "What?"

"You're doing it again."

I tap the notebook with my pen. "This?" I lower my voice to a whisper. "Eventually, someone's going to get Konstantin. You know who gets the least jail time? People with evidence." I tap the notebook again, once for each syllable. "Ev. I. Dence."

Sash rolls her eyes. "That's not what I mean."

"Huh. I don't know what you're talking about." *Only, I totally do.*

"That Jedi mind trick you played with Igor--I know what it is." She bobs her brows. "I'm telling you, it's vampire power."

I pinch the bridge of my nose. "Not again."

"Look, vampires make humans feel afraid, unaware, or turned on. You conjure *'I'm invisible magic'* like a pro."

"Vampires do not exist, Sash." I can't help the edge to my voice. For some reason, it always bugs me when Sash brings up vampires. "I'm just the school's resident nut job. It makes me easy to overlook."

"Igor wouldn't care about Chemistry class. The guy loves computers, same as you do. I think if you showed a little interest, he'd notice you."

"Igor plays *Call of Duty* online. I track public websites for shipping and receiving data about the Port Authority. Not the same thing, trust me."

Now, it's Sash's turn to lower her voice. "You don't have to hide, Lexa. Everyone's forgotten about Chemistry class."

"Not Mr. Brookhollow."

"Maybe not him, but all the kids have." Sash sets her hand on my forearm. "People need to know how lovely you are."

"Thanks." I can't help but smile. Sash knows just what to say.

With that, I let my guard down. Which is the only explanation for what happens next. Since I stop focusing on being invisible, the worst kid in school slides onto the bench before us.

Vice. Short for Viceroy. What a dick.

Vice is that kid who looks like trouble, skips school constantly, and no one calls him on it. Ever. He's got a long face, overly large eyes, spiked-up hair, and a pointy chin. Vice even sports some rune tattoos on his neck. His parents work for Konstantin at the Port Authority along with my father, so I guess that explains the face ink.

"How's it going, sugar tits?" asks Vice.

"Don't talk to my sister that way," I warn.

"I'm not talking to Sash." Vice bobs his brows and leers in my direction. "I can tell what you're packing under that muu muu."

I roll my eyes. "Don't you have somewhere else to be?"

"Why? Am I vanishing from sight?" asks Vice. "Or, am I turning a different color?" Vice calls out to the bus. "Lexa's seeing shit again! Watch out!"

Sadly, the bus goes quiet and everyone looks at me and Sash. My heart sinks.

"Ha, ha," I deadpan. "I've never heard that one before."

An evil smile rounds Vice's mouth. "Need to hear something new? How about we discuss your sister?" He coughs right at me and Sash. The meaning is clear; *Sash is sick.*

"Watch it," I warn.

"Your skin looks so pale, sister Sash," says Vice with mock sympathy. "And the dark circles under your eyes get worse by the day. Make sure your parents lock down your life insurance policy because, damn."

Rage rises within me. "Back off. Now."

Vice smirks. He came over here to get me angry. *Mission Accomplished.*

Thankfully, the bus pulls over. It's our stop. Sash and I take off while making a point of ignoring Vice.

Once we're off the bus, it's a short hike to reach the main

gates to our driveway. These mark the only one way in or out, considering how our house is surrounded by a ten-foot high wall. Basically, the place screams, *mafia inside.*

After we stroll past the gate, it's another trek to hit the front door. Our house is a two-story brick building with white pillars. We step up to the entrance, where two security guys let us inside. The house interior is notable for its blandness. There's nothing personal in here at all. It's like living in a generic department store display called Middle-Class White People.

After the unpleasantness with Vice, I'm looking forward to hiding out in my room for a while. That doesn't happen. The moment Sash and I are inside, we can hear our parents yelling in the kitchen. My sister and I pause.

"You've been stealing from Konstantin?" asks Mom. "Do you have a death wish?"

"Everyone skims," says Dad. "That's business."

"Shh," says Mom. "The girls are home." She steps into the main hallway between the entrance and kitchen, which is where Sash and I stand. Today, Mom wears a blue dress with a matching neckerchief. "There you are, kids! Welcome home! Now, go to your rooms and do your homework. I'll let you know when dinner's ready."

"Is everything okay?" I ask.

"It's all fine," says Mom. "As a matter of fact, the big worry here is you." Mom angles her head toward the kitchen. "Isn't that right, honey?"

Dad steps out to stand beside Mom. He wraps his arm around her shoulder in a move that always makes me think they're posing for a catalog picture. "Yes, Legacy Day is coming up, isn't it?"

I stifle a groan. Legacy Day is a tradition at Paxton High. All the seniors give a presentation on someone they admire. The *comrade kids* always talk about Konstantin.

"Yeah, I'm working on it." I shoot them a thumbs up.

Mom adjusts her neckerchief again. She only does that when she's really upset. "Your father and I think you should talk about Konstantin's philanthropy. That should give you a different angle than everyone else."

"Konstantin never misses Legacy Day," adds Dad. "It's important we impress him this year."

Because you're stealing from the guy.

"And be sure to draw him as part of your presentation," adds Mom. "You're such a talented artist."

I force a smile. "I'll come up with something great, I promise."

Sash steps into the kitchen. "Mom! Dad!" Her voice echoes into the hallway. "There's something I need to show you."

Here's why my sister is the best. She's purposefully distracting my parents so I can sneak away. And Sash is the kind of liar who's so sincere, no one suspects what's she's really up to.

I am one lucky girl.

But I've learned my lesson about letting my guard down. As I slip off for my bedroom, I repeat my favorite phrase.

I'm invisible. I'm invisible. I'm invisible.

8

CAELIN

MORE THAN A THOUSAND YEARS OLD

M anhattan, seven years ago

6:32 a.m.

I march along Fifth Avenue. My goal? Another day of illegal activity at my company, Empire Investments.

And when I say illegal, I mean that from the human standpoint. Vampires don't hold to any laws but our own, and I've broken none of those.

The sky lightens with the first touch of sunrise. Vehicles stream up and down the street. The scent of old perfume and new exhaust fills the air. I approach a bland-looking skyscraper, the headquarters of my company, Empire Investments. My routine is to arrive early and leave late. Playing around with numbers is my distraction and solace.

No friends.

No relationships.

No problems.

I enter the building and take the private elevator up to my

offices. I use three chambers. First, there's outer reception. Second, I have a private meeting room. And third, there's the place where I actually work: my inner office.

I enter reception first. It's a lot of oak paneling, expensive rugs, and hand-carved everything. My Vice President of Human Resources sits behind a large desk. *Prudence MacGuire.* Like always, her red hair is pulled back into a prim bun. She wears far too much make-up along with a fitted tweed suit.

And it's all a lie.

Prudence is Russian, not Scottish. But when it comes to humans, I feel more comfortable after I know their lies, so long as they still get things done. And Prudence is very efficient.

"Good morning, Prudence."

She bows her head. "Your Majesty." Prudence knows enough about my true identity to get her job done, nothing more.

"You shouldn't be in this early. We need a personal assistant to sit behind this desk."

"Of course," lies Prudence. "I'll get on that right away."

She never does, though. For me, it's a matter of curiosity as to how long Prudence will keep up the pretense. After a thousand years of living, I have a limited set of interests when it comes to humans. One is tracking their capacity to lie. Every time I think I've found the bottom of that particular well, they surprise me.

I step up to a wall panel that's really the entrance to my meeting room. "Is he here?"

No question who *'he'* is in this scenario. It's a soldier from the Italian mob. Even after all these years, construction remains firmly in their grasp. And since I've decided to fund building Konstantin's latest clubs, I must deal with them.

Time was, I allowed Konstantin to parlay directly with the Italian mob. Let's just say the clean-up became too cumbersome. Humans are weak, but what they lack in strength, they more than make up for in numbers. So far, vampires are little more than fairy tales. I plan to keep it that way.

The door swings open. I step through the small hallway that leads to my meeting room. The thin passage soon opens to a wide space with oak paneling and leather chairs.

A man sits there. He's a scrawny guy with slicked-back hair, tanned skin, and far too much cologne. "I'm Joey." He smoothes the lapels of his shiny gray suit. "We need to talk."

No conversation with a member of the Italian mob ends well when it begins in this manner. Even so, I'm curious. I take a seat across from him. "Go on."

"I do the books, ya know? It's a lot of internet stuff."

"You're a hacker."

"Nothing like what Konstantin's guys can do, but I'm good. You paid us in unmarked bills for some construction work."

"It was legitimate work on two new clubs where Konstantin and I are part-owners. You were the ones who wanted cash."

If it were up to me, I'd never buy a dance club, let alone pay for construction in cash. But Konstantin loves the idea and I made a promise to his sister. The rest is history.

"I was looking around and I found some things. You've got billions loaded in offshore accounts. No one should have that kind of money."

"Clearly, I do."

"Want to know what I think?" Joey goes on without waiting for any approval. "The rumors are all true. You're some kind of supernatural guy. Maybe even a vampire."

"Yet, here we are, speaking during the daytime."

"Eh, I still think I'm right. You're a bloodsucker."

"So, you want a payment for your discretion?"

"Yeah."

"Nae."

"In that case, I gotta tell ya." He reaches under his jacket and pulls out a pistol, complete with a silencer. "I can't look away while you rob humanity blind."

"I suppose not." I lean back in my leather chair. "Go on. Attack. I'll even give you the first shot."

Joey aims the weapon and fires directly into my heart. It hurts like hell, but it won't kill me. Blood pools across my jacket.

I rise. "Nice shot. Bad plan."

Joey pales. "What's happening?"

"Don't you read? You can only kill vampires with a stake." I pull out an obelisk dagger from under my jacket. "Like this one." I toss the weapon so it lands right in the human's heart. "And that's how you do it."

The man slumps forward in his chair. I leave him to bleed out while I head through another hidden door at the back of the meeting chamber. This one leads to my inner office. I enter the room.

Unlike the first two chambers, this final space is all shiny steel and black granite. I approach my desk, which sits against the left wall. Taking my seat, I soak in my favorite view: New York city's skyline as shown through the massive window that serves as the center wall. The right wall of the room is covered in monitors.

Looking down, I inspect the many buttons embedded into the surface of my desk. After pressing one, the displays flare to life.

Konstantin's face covers the entire wall. In some ways, he looks as he did when I first met him: strong jawline, tanned skin, large brown eyes, and blue tattoos along his neck. Over the years, he's added a few things to his appearance, such as a broken nose and two scars through his left eyebrow. Still, there remains a certain energy about him that I envy. Somehow, Konstantin always seems ready for battle, even though everyone we truly fought for is gone.

"Good morning, Caelin."

I skip the pleasantries. "Did you tip off an Italian mobster about my business, perhaps in order to pay off a debt?"

Konstantin grins. "I figured you needed the battle practice. How did you do it?"

"Obelisk dagger to the heart," I reply.

"Always a good choice."

"You're cleaning up the body. Send your crew over here."

"*My* crew? Where are *your* bloodkin?"

By this, Konstantin means Hunter and the others from the old days.

"They aren't here," I reply. "And even if they were, I don't make them clean up after your mistakes."

"All right. But you owe me a favor."

I chuckle. "Not a chance. You sent a human here who might have killed me."

Konstantin shoots me his most winning smile. "It's like this. I'm a great businessman, but not the best."

"You don't say."

Konstantin loves the thrill of the heist. There's no adrenaline hit if you don't need the money, so he keeps himself almost penniless. It's the only way someone can live a thousand years and still have an empty bank account.

Konstantin grins. "You see, this week is the annual Legacy Day at Paxton High."

I stifle a groan. "Oh, no. Not again."

"Come on, all my best capos have family at that school. The kids present on their favorite person… and I get an inside view to their parent's minds."

"You get your ass kissed, that's what happens."

"Honestly, I could use your expertise about who I should kill."

"Konstantin, I am not going to a gymnasium in New Jersey to hear a bunch of humans talk about how amazing you are. And I'm not helping you kill anyone."

"Hey, some of them are stealing from me."

"Which ones?"

"The Alekhins, for starters. They've been working at the Port Authority." He bobs his brows.

"You say the names like I should know who you're talking about."

"Prudence's little brother is living with the Alekhins. A kid called Vice."

"Oh, I've heard about them. Grigory and Mila Alekhin. Prudence hates them. She wants her kid brother in the city with her. How much did they steal?"

"Three hundred million," says Konstantin.

I sniff. "I'd kill them, too. Just leave the kid alive. When the Alekhins are done, I'll set up Vice in the city for Prudence."

Konstantin winks. "What, no *thank you*? I didn't have to check with you before ending them, you know. And there are others to worry about as well."

"This Legacy Day sounds worse by the moment."

"Honestly, I could use your help. There's another guy who's stealing from me, Mikhail. Only I'm not sure if I'll ice him or not. He didn't skim as much. What do you think?"

These conversations can go on for hours if I'm not careful.

"Goodbye, Konstantin." I press a button on my desk. The wall of monitors goes dark.

Sometimes, I really wish I'd never made that vow to Elisava.

9

LEXA

*I*t's almost my turn at Legacy Day. *Shoot me now.*

I pace backstage at my high school auditorium. Every so often, I peep through the velvet side curtains and out into the audience. My sister and mother sit in the front row. Both wear pink sundresses, only Mom's also sporting her ever-present neckerchief. Dad's off doing *whatever it is* that he does for Konstantin.

I pull at my neckline so hard, I pop a few stitches on the shoulder seams of my own sundress. Mine's purple, by the way. And although I gave in to Mom about wearing the dress, I paired it with my Doc Martens, so there's that.

On center stage, my classmate, Tanya, stands behind a podium, talking about the awesomeness that is Konstantin King. Beside her, there's a big screen displaying the photo of a truly horrible sculpture of Konstantin's head.

Tanya finishes up to some light applause. One of my teachers taps me on the shoulder. "You're next, Lexa."

"Thanks." I step out on stage, and pause before the podium. "My name is Alexa Uznetsov. The person I want to talk about today is my sister, Sasha."

In the front row, Sash beams. At the same time, Mom gasps—she thought I'd talk about Konstantin. Dad is MIA, so he can't glare at me now. No doubt, I'll get my share of death stares from him later.

"Sasha?" asks someone in the audience. "Don't you mean *plague girl?*"

I scan the crowd. Sure enough, my heckler is Vice. My blood heats with anger.

From the front row, Mom twiddles her fingers at me. It's a hand signal between us. Mom is acting like she's a puppeteer who's pulling strings. It means Bratva are in the house and I must follow the rules.

Act submissive.
Don't make eye contact.
Be invisible.

But there's playing along, and then there's Vice calling Lexa the plague girl. None of the teachers are doing anything, either. I inspect the room once more. The reason why becomes clear.

Konstantin King is here, looking like a mash-up of a man mountain, biker, and serial killer. Vice's parents are two of Konstantin's top captains. For some reason, Konstantin wears a silent smile as Vice mouths off. That's basically an unspoken approval of the kid's nastiness. No one will step in now.

Think, Lexa.

I memorized this speech because it counts toward my graduation. Now, I can't remember where I left off. I lean toward the microphone. "Picture, please."

Two drawings of Sasha appear on the screen beside me. "This is my art project for this presentation. I chose the topic, My Loved One Through Time. On the left, you can see Sasha as a kid. On the right, I drew her as she is today."

The left drawing was inspired by some baby I found on the

internet. Sash and I don't have any pics from when we were growing up. Trouble is, I selected my topic late. My Loved One Through Time was the only thing left. So, I had to make stuff up. Both images are pretty, although the grown-up Sash does look a little pale.

"Call the coroner." That's Vice again.

My entire body vibrates with fury. Over on the front row, Sash stares at her lap. Even though I can't see her face, there's no missing how her shoulders tremble. She's crying.

I glare at the far corner of the auditorium, where Vice is sitting with his overlarge eyes and spiked-up hair. The little freak is smiling his face off.

"Zip it, loser," I call.

"Make me," counters Vice.

I'm about to cross the auditorium and punch Vice in the eye when Mom clears her throat. My mother's now frantically twiddling her fingers while mouthing the name, *Konstantin*. That snaps me out of the worst of my fury.

Right. I just need to get through this presentation and I'll graduate. Vice wants me to lose my temper.

I gesture toward the screen and force a smile. "My sister, Sash, loves to read."

"Because that's about all she can handle." That's Vice yet again. This time, some of his buddies chuckle.

Sash sobs aloud. Rage careens through me. My mind blanks. I totally lose it. Random facts have been percolating in my head for months. Now, they align in new ways. Fury helps me focus on the perfect comeback for this douche.

I lean in closer to the microphone. "At least my parents don't route cargo to New York harbor when the place is red hot with law enforcement. Ever heard of Boston? They haven't had cargo seized in six months. Dumbasses."

A charged kind of silence fills the auditorium. Mom's shoulders slump. Sash looks paler than usual. Konstantin stares at me with an unreadable look.

That's when I realize my mistake. Vice's father works alongside Dad. If there's bad stuff happening at New York harbor, then both of them could get in trouble. Even if it's really someone else fault, Konstantin might think my father should have noticed.

Oh, damn.

10

LEXA

*H*ours later, Sash and I lie on my bedroom floor and stare at the ceiling. For some reason, the two of us are always more comfortable on the ground. Go figure.

Suddenly, I'm not in my room anymore. Sash and I rest outside on the frozen earth beneath some towering pine trees.

My heart sinks. *Damn, I'm having another hallucination.*

Sash and I are much younger. Snowflakes land on us. I hold a small pendant and contemplate a path through the woods.

But to where?

I shake my head, snapping myself out of the vision. A moment later, I'm back in my bedroom. Any illusion of a winter forest is gone. I exhale. This is exactly what Mr. Brookhollow warned me about. When I'm stressed, I have hallucinations. I just need to talk to him about it. Eventually, they'll go away.

"It's not your fault," says Sash. "You know that, right?"

"It's totally my fault," I counter.

Some version of this conversation has been going on for hours. After taking down Vice, I walked offstage without finishing my speech. Mom dropped us off at home and drove away. At the time, the house was empty. And it's stayed that way ever since. Sash and I are still waiting for some word from either of our parents.

Nothing yet.

"If anything, it's Vice's fault," clarifies Sash.

"Good point. That little dirtbag was lurking in the back of the audience. He *had* to know Konstantin was there. Vice was trying to get a rise out of me and humiliate Dad in front of his boss."

"That boy just wants attention." Sash rolls over on her side and faces me. "Hey, where did you come up with that stuff about New York and Boston?"

"Oh, that. There are websites where you can track that stuff." I wince. "I shouldn't have gotten so obsessed with Konstantin's business."

"No, you did the right thing. We still might get into a witness protection program or something."

It's after one o'clock in the morning when my mother bursts into the room. That part isn't so shocking—Mom never knocks. But, her hair's a mess. Mascara runs down one side of Mom's face. And her neckerchief is askew.

"It's over," announces Mom. "We're moving to New York."

"Was it because of what I said today?"

"Yes, it is," confirms Mom. Those three words are like so many knives to my heart. "And we're lucky. The Alekhins got it worse."

"Does that mean Vice?" asks Sash. *Because she's nice that way.*

"No," says Mom. "He'll move in with his sister somewhere."

"And his parents?" I ask.

"They got into a sedan after Legacy Day," answers Mom. "I don't expect them to see them again."

Sash sniffs. "Is Dad…"

"Dead?" finishes Mom. "No, he wasn't at Legacy Day, as you may have noticed. While we were watching presentations, your father skipped town."

I sit upright, my mind spinning through options. "Maybe we could run, too."

Sash sits up as well. "Yeah. We should go right now."

"That's not possible," says Mom. "Konstantin has an 'in' at Silver Pharma. That's how we got into this secret drug trial in the first place. If we run, that's the end of Sash's meds."

I slump my shoulders. "This is all my fault," I say.

"That it is," confirms Mom yet again. "And now, you'll fix things. Konstantin wants you to work for a man named Otto in New York."

My mind blanks. "What about school?"

"You're done with it," declares Mom. "And Sash will get home-schooled." She rounds on me. "Your insolence got us in trouble, but your father's thieving may have saved everything."

"I don't understand," says Sash.

"Your father stole from Konstantin. Now, we have a twenty-three million dollar debt to pay off. I convinced Konstantin that you have a big mouth but good surveillance skills. Do that recon-naissance stuff you did at the presentation—all that junk about harbors—only a lot more of it. If you keep paying off the debt, that will keep us alive, thanks to me."

My mind tries to process all that's happening. "Dad skimmed twenty-three million?"

"He's been moving the cash into offshore accounts. Your father's been planning to leave us for some time." Mom sighs. "You'll work for a man named Otto. He's one of Konstantin's soldiers." She twiddles her fingers. "Only, remember to play the puppet game. What is it, girls?"

Sash and I reply in unison. "Act submissive. Don't make eye contact. Be invisible."

I make some quick calculations. "If I just made Konstantin millions, then we'll pay off the debt in no time, right?"

"Your cut is fifty-thousand," explains Mom. "Otto will give you what's left over, after he takes out his fees."

For some reason, I can only repeat what Mom says. "Fees."

"We need money to live in New York," says Mom. "Rent. Food. Meds. Congratulations, you're now the wage earner for the household."

"I'll never pay that much off." My stomach sinks. "I must speak to Konstantin directly."

"Don't you dare," says Mom. "I got us this deal... and it wasn't easy." She points to the closet. "Both of you, grab your suitcases. Konstantin wants us gone in an hour."

"What? Why?" I do a double-take. "This is our house."

"No, Konstantin owns everything," says Mom. "And he could also have our heads if he wanted them. Believe me, we're lucky. Now, get packing." She trudges out of the room and slams the door behind her.

A heavy silence hangs in the air. My chest feels tight with worry and shock.

"It'll be fine," says Sash. "And I meant what I said before. This isn't your fault."

My throat constricts with grief. I'd wanted to go to college and become a detective. Or maybe an artist. Now, all that's over. Sash says this isn't my fault. But in the end, it doesn't really matter whether I'm guilty or not.

I'm still sentenced to pay.

CAELIN

I stand in my penthouse window and watch storm clouds roll in over the Hudson River. Vessels stream into the city. Night falls.

My reflection seems to stare back at me from the window pane. I appear as little more than an outline. *How fitting.* I once stood atop my stone castle and watched ships approach my realm. That man had purpose.

How long has it been since I watched the ocean and felt anything but numb?

The opening notes of Vivaldi's *The Four Seasons* echo through my apartment. It's my ring tone for Hunter.

"Computer, accept call," I state.

Hunter's voice sounds just as it did a thousand years ago. The edge of excitement and humor is unmistakable. "Hello, Caelin."

"How are things in India?"

"The Gray Woman is at it again. We found another enhanced human."

"The same injection marks?"

"Aye," replies Hunter. "There's the mark of an infinity loop on the wrist."

These marks are a series of needle pricks that scar over into a looping figure eight. That means you're a test subject for none other than the Gray Woman... who's now reinvented herself as Dr. Gray, CEO of Silver Pharma. These days, the Gray Woman is mixing her magic with modern technology in order to enhance humans with vampire powers. It's a classic move to insert chaos into the world.

I thought humans and the Gray Woman would save my people. How wrong I was.

"What's this injection for?" There are three types of enhancements based on vampire DNA: extra strength, the ability to inspire fear, or the power to convince others you're invisible.

"This was one of the injections that gives extra strength," answers Hunter. "That's not the big news, however. The Gray Woman also dug up a primal elemental, took samples, and reset it into the ground." Hunter lowers his voice. "This one's a mindlock daemon."

My brows lift. "That has the magical ability to cause hallucinations."

"Aye. After we found the mindlock, we thought we'd sailed around the world. Two days passed before we realized we never left the same cave."

"If the Gray Woman is targeting primal daemons, we better keep track of who she digs up and what they do. No doubt, she's working on a new set of injections and enhancements. Keep me posted."

As the line goes dead, the door to my penthouse swings open. Only one person enters here without knocking. Sure enough, in the window's reflection, I see Konstantin step into the room. He holds a bottle of Scotch whiskey in his right hand.

Konstantin plunks onto the black leather couch behind me. "Thought you'd want company."

"You don't have to do this," I say.

"Yeah, I do." Konstantin opens the bottle. "You and I are the only two who remember her."

No question who he means here. Elisava.

I step over to a side table, grab a few glasses, and bring them to Konstantin.

"How did it go at Paxton High?" I ask.

Konstantin fills the two glasses. "I killed the Alekhins. As promised, I didn't touch the kid, Vice."

"Thanks. I'll move him to the city."

"The last one, Mikhail, ran off. One of his kids, Alexa, will pay off the debt."

I take a sip of whiskey. "How can you be sure?"

Konstantin finishes his glass in one gulp. "I'm an excellent judge of character."

I chuckle. "This sounds like another *get rich quick* scheme."

Konstantin refills his glass. "Eventually, one of them will work. Then, I'll never ask you for cash again, you skinflint Scottish bastard."

"At least, you have goals."

"Da." Konstantin downs a second glass of whiskey. "Alexa will be a good investment, mark my words. But she stays secret. I'll only talk to her through a cut-out, this guy named Otto. And he'll keep her apart from the rest of my organization. That means you, too."

"I've already forgotten her name." I return my focus to the window. A light summer rain falls over the city and harbor.

Minutes pass before I speak again.

"Elisava and I met on a night like this. There was a sweet summer storm. A Rus ship came to our shores, wanting to trade prisoners. I released someone from the dungeons."

"Pyotr the Bold."

"Aye. Then, the Rus brought their prisoner to my court. We expected one of our own to come back. But, when the cloak came away, I found Elisava instead. She requested refuge; I couldn't refuse. That's how she escaped Fyodor, you know. Elisava simply asked for help. A group of Rus brought her to my shores."

"That's how she was," says Konstantin. "A purer soul was never born."

"My people wanted to kill her on the spot." Konstantin growls; he hates this part of the story. "Yet, I knew right away I could never let anyone hurt her. And I married her. My people grew to love her, just as I did."

Konstantin sighs. "Want to hit some of our clubs? If I sit here and keep listening to you, I'll stake myself."

"Not my speed."

"You can't just stand around and mope over my sister for eternity."

I shrug. "It's worked for the last thousand years."

"Hey, remember our first Norse raid? You killed all those nightling in the shallows."

"Hard to forget."

"A few of my creations have gone rogue. I've got nightlings hiding out in the Hudson River."

"Do I even want to know how long they've been there?"

"Long enough. Want to help me with killing and clean up? And before you start lecturing me, even your nightlings go rogue sometimes."

I pull out the obelisk dagger from its holster under my suit jacket. "That could be interesting."

"Good. I'm driving. I just bought a new fleet of Hummers."

Classic Konstantin. He must have pulled in a recent influx of cash. He tries to spend it as soon as he makes it. That keeps the stakes for his heists high and his adrenaline pumping.

I suppose I do have one friend, after all. And I'm fortunate it's Konstantin.

PRESENT DAY

LEXA

TWENTY-FOUR YEARS OLD

M *anhattan, present day*

Another Saturday night, another stakeout.

This time, I'm watching Ghost, a thief who just filled his walk-in safe with ill-gotten gold. It's my job to stakeout the guy's apartment, which is in a high-rise called the Nouveau Palais. Once I get enough info, I'll write up an attack plan. After that, Otto's team do their thing and I take my cut.

I've been waiting in this coffee shop for hours. There's been no sign of Ghost yet. That doesn't worry me, though. The key to this job is patience.

Suddenly, my phone blares the *Imperial March* from Star Wars. I stifle the urge to groan. That's the ring tone of my boss, Otto. He's a middle-aged guy with a beer gut, receding hairline, and iron-fisted grip on my lady balls. *Long story.*

I pop in my ear buds and click *accept*. "It's Lexa."

"What the fuck?" Otto's gravelly voice blares in my ears. "I can hardly hear you."

"I'm in Big Apple Coffee." The place looks like it fell out of the 1950's... and didn't land too nicely. In other words, Big Apple sports dingy walls, a grimy tile floor, and chipped Formica tables.

"Why can't you run a stakeout from someplace that's quiet?" asks Otto. "You know, like a normal person?"

"I don't know," I counter. "Why can't *you* text instead of call? You know, like someone from this century?"

A few seconds later, my phone dings with an alert. *Probably a text from Otto.* I should know better than to look, but I've never been the type who knows better about anything.

I take a peep.

It's a drawing of me as a pin-up girl from the 1940's. Which isn't too far off. I'm on the shorter side with lots of curves. I don't dress in pin-up style, though—no push-up bras and bright colors for me, thank you very much. With my job, it's best to blend in. Today, that means a pencil skirt and white top. Unlike this image on my phone which shows me bare-ass naked.

Ugh. What an Otto thing to do.

"The pic is good from the shoulders on up," I say dryly. The artist captured my heart-shaped face, ice-blue eyes, and long brown hair.

Otto snickers. "One of the *club shlubs* left this under my door."

Club shlubs. That's what we call the gents who visit Otto's Lucky Ladies Lounge And Exotic Dancing Club. It's a horrible name, but Otto is known for hiring great strippers, not having excellent writing skills. I live in the club's back room and participate in the odd bikini contest for extra cash. Fan art is a sad side effect.

I really shouldn't have looked.

"You can't send me this stuff, Otto. It's so illegal, it isn't funny."

"Then grab a cop, *Lexa*. Tell 'em how I gave you trouble while you're staking out some criminal, all so I can rob the guy's safe... and you can work off your debt to the Russian mob. If the police get suspicious, just whine about your sick sister again."

Wow. Talking about Sash is really low. And it's almost as rude as pointing out how I can never go to the police. Some girls inherit trust funds from their fathers. I get old mafia debt. To pay my bills, I do surveillance gigs for Otto as well as the odd bikini contest.

All of which is why Otto has me by the lady balls. Konstantin trusts him to make regular payments on *'my'* debt. There's no way I can leave his employment without a better source of money as well as a new connection for Sash's meds. And even if a new job like this existed, why would they hire me? My mob ties make me radioactive.

The walls of the coffee shop seem to press in around me. I'm twenty-four and this is as good as my life will get. And I can't run. Sash won't survive without her meds. Suddenly, it feels hard to breathe.

"Talk." demands Otto. "Give me an update."

"I'll deliver what I promised you by next Friday. Sandwich and Cookies."

Since I fear the FBI, I speak in code. The 'S' in Sandwich stands for a Schedule of my target's activities. The 'C' of Cookies means Combination... as in the way to open the bedroom safe.

And this is why Ghost is a cosmic dumbass. *Who keeps a safe-o-gold in his bedroom?* It's like asking to get robbed. If anything, the guy's lucky I'm making a schedule of when he's out of town so no one gets killed during the break-in.

"Next Friday," repeats Otto. "You're sure?"

I sniff. "Do I ever fail you?"

"Do I ever trust anyone?" counters Otto.

"Let me put it to you this way," I reply. "I'm in this noisy cafe because it's got the perfect view of the apartment building in question. Got it?"

The line goes dead. That's the closest I get to a *'you go girl'* or *'have a nice night'* from Otto. Leaning back in my chair, I run the numbers for the millionth time. There are no other options. I'm stuck with Otto for the rest of my life.

The walls press in even more closely. I pull on the neckline of my shirt, trying to get in more oxygen.

Out on the sidewalk, an elderly couple pauses by the coffee shop's bay window. The distraction is so welcome, I could cheer. The man sets down an old-time fedora with the brim upwards-- the classic sign of a street performer about to do their thing.

Next, the couple brings out violins and play *Pachabel's Canon*. The music is slow-paced and romantic. Chances are, these two aren't in this for the money. Which is good, since no one's thrown them so much as a dime yet. Instead, they're enjoying each other's gifts and company.

That's almost as beautiful as the music itself.

I sigh. What a sweet break from my dismal future. Sadly, I'm the only one who seems to notice their performance. The rest of the coffee shop stays packed and noisy. Out on the street, pedestrians stride past the musicians without a second thought.

Finally, another man pauses on the sidewalk. This isn't just any guy, mind you, but Caelin MacGregor, the so-called King of Empire Investments. Rumors are, Caelin is ruthless in business and a bastard in general. I believe those tales. Then there are other whispers. Folks say Caelin is a vampire with mind control powers. I have a different opinion on that.

What a load of B-S.

Caelin pauses to watch the musicians, giving me a chance to inspect him more closely. To say that Caelin is *just handsome* is like declaring that the Mona Lisa is *simply a painting*.

The slightest shiver rolls across Caelin's shoulders. Inch by inch, he turns toward me. My pulse skyrockets. Our gazes meet.

Everything goes haywire.

Lights flash in the coffee shop. Street lamps pulse and crackle. A breeze strikes up out of nowhere. Mist pours across the floor. An electric shock of worry moves through my limbs.

There can only be one explanation. I'm having another hallucination, just like Chemistry class back in Paxton High.

There's been one big bonus of working for Otto. I haven't had an hallucination since I left New Jersey. And I certainly never saw moist or flashing lights before.

This can't be good.

CAELIN

MORE THAN A THOUSAND YEARS OLD

*M*anhattan, present day

Another night, another potential mess from Konstantin.

My friend has a soldier staking out the apartment of an infamous criminal named Ghost. For a long list of reasons, I want to check this out for myself. Something about this heist doesn't feel right.

And I made a promise to keep Konstantin alive.

It's past nightfall when I walk over to the apartment building where this fellow lives. It's a place called the Nouveau Palais. I own the building. In fact, this hi-rise is one of the best in my real estate portfolio. Across the street, fluorescent light shines out from a run-down cafe.

I make a mental note to buy this coffee shop and put in a Starbucks. Big Apple Coffee is bringing the whole neighborhood down.

For a long moment, I wait on the sidewalk. Ghost's apartment looms across the street. Some street musicians play *Pachabel's*

Canon. The sky darkens.

And I lock gazes with Alexa Uznetsov.

I kept my word. Although I've never spoken her name since, I know Miss Uznetsov has become Konstantin's top-secret money maker. The man hasn't asked me for a loan in years.

She's clever, sure. Still, she's only a human. Impermanent. Unimportant.

So why can't I look away?

Link by link, an invisible chain of connection forms between us. Energy pulses. Spirits align. Suddenly, I sense her soul as if it's my own. Without consciously willing it, my fangs descend.

Forming an unconscious link with a stranger is bad enough. What happens next is beyond imagining.

The world alters.

Street lights flash. Mist rolls in. Cars vanish from the asphalt. Pedestrians disappear. Haze twines up my body. When the mist vanishes, I'm no longer standing on the sidewalk.

I'm inside Big Apple Coffee. Alexa Uznetsov sits on the tabletop before me. Her legs are parted. I stand between her thighs. Up close, Alexa Uznetsov is an entirely new experience.

Face to face, I soak in more about this woman. She exudes ferocity and passion. Desire spikes as I soak in the petal-pink shade of her lips... The delicious curves of her chest... And the intensity of her ice-blue eyes. Her scent—cedar and musk—fills my every pore. My body responds. Fire heats my veins.

I want this woman.

Her correct name appears in my mind.

Not Alexa. It's Lexa.

Part of me warns that I should worry. I've somehow transported into a random coffee shop. Now, I'm being overwhelmed by a stranger's presence. Could this be an hallucination or, even worse, a spell? Did the Gray Woman enhance this human with the power of that mindlink daemon?

I should care. I don't. The lines of connection between us deepen. Nothing else matters.

It's Lexa who breaks the silence. "Do you know why this is happening?"

There's only one response here. The truth.

"Nae, lass."

Lexa's mouth falls open. A mixture of fire and steel shines in her eyes. The connection between us frays. I feel the growing distance as sharply as if it were a knife.

Lexa looks away. The cord between us fully snaps. My soul sinks.

Light flashes. Fresh mist rolls in. Everything alters once more.

Suddenly, I'm outside again. The pedestrians, street lights, and cars are all back in place. Lexa's returned to her window-side seat. She stares intently at her cell phone. Moments ago, a link pulsed between us. Now, there's nothing. I walk away.

All of which brings me to where I am now, and that's strolling back toward my office building. All my thoughts focus on a single question.

What. Was. That?

The Gray Woman is still digging up primal daemons. Hunter leads a team that keeps track of what powers are in these creatures—abilities that the Gray Woman could inject into humans. Lexa could be enhanced with the powers of a mindlock daemon.

For some reason, another option appears.

Fated mates. Could that be what's happening?

As soon as the question enters my mind, my heart cracks with grief. In every way that matters, Elisava is still my fated mate. Lexa may have a few odd powers, but she remains a human.

Centuries passed as I waited for the Gray Woman and humanity to bring back bloodkin women. If it were going to happen, it would have taken place long ago. Sadly, Elisava was my first and only chance at happiness.

Another option appears. Lexa could be reacting to my

vampire nature. And I know how this attraction will end. *Red madness.*

For too long, I've been watching the Gray Woman and assuming her magic can't cause too much trouble. I was wrong. Whatever is happening, it's definitely serious. I need my best people on it.

I pull out my phone and dial Hunter. Like always, my second in command never wastes time with greetings.

"She's still at it," states Hunter. "These days, the Gray Woman is using her water elemental power to pop over from New York and appear near some caves outside Calcutta. She sampled another primal daemon last week. We just dug it up. A Soul Piercer. Nasty."

"How long do you need to return to New York?"

"A week, minimum. Indigo and the Edwards will need to finish things up for me. That won't be easy."

"I'd like you back in New York within seventy-two hours."

Hunter chuckles. "Who are you and what have you done with Caelin MacGregor?"

I know what he means. I haven't had a fire in my belly for anything in centuries. My friend wants an answer. I'm not willing to give one.

"Just be on time."

I hang up.

14

LEXA

S ure, I'm sitting in Big Apple Coffee. Still, in some ways, it's as if I'm back in Mr. Brookhollow's office at Paxton High. I pore over every millisecond of what just happened, it's as if I'm experiencing it all over again.

Everything in the coffee shop goes dark, except for a few beams of moonlight. Moments pass as my eyes adjust. Once I can see clearly again, I can't believe what's around me. The cafe is empty. The street outside is deserted as well. The entire city appears dark and abandoned.

And I've changed, too. Now I'm sitting on the tabletop with my skirt up and legs parted. A man towers before me.

It's Caelin MacGregor.

Maybe I should scream or run for the exit, but I don't. Instead, my entire being seems frozen in shock... Except for my ability to soak in more details of Caelin MacGregor. Up close, this so-called king of Empire Investments is even more magnetic. A gentle scruff lines his chin. His face is framed with strong bone structure. His full lips appear ripe for a kiss. The gentle scent of spice and leather assaults me. It isn't fair for this man to be gorgeous and smell good as well.

All this time, Caelin has been staring at me with a look that can only be described as worshipful hunger. Don't get me wrong. I make side money in bikini contests. Getting ogled is nothing new. But I've never been visually devoured in the way that's happening right now. The sheer intensity of his stare makes my core twist with desire. With every cell in my body, I want to touch the curl of hair at the base of Caelin's neck. Some part of me screams that this whole situation is impossible. More of me doesn't care.

Somehow, I manage to speak.

"Do you know why this is happening?"

"Nae, lass."

I'd read in the tabloids how Caelin has a Scottish accent. But knowing that as a fact and hearing it in his voice? Those are two very different experiences. The man is nothing less than hypnotic. My blood heats. Excitement skitters across my skin. All I can focus on is the gentle itch of Caelin's pants against my inner thigh.

His gaze... his body... this connection... it's all so perfect.

And somehow, that changes things.

Before, my practical side echoed in the far reaches of my brain, urging me to run for the exit. The warning did not get through. But now? Logic returns to my lust-filled brain. This wonderful moment with Caelin doesn't happen to girls like me. And that leads to a realization.

None of this is real.

As if in response, the lights flash faster than ever before. A breeze strikes up out of nowhere. The last of the strange mist gets whisked away.

The next thing I know, everything is back to the way it was five minutes ago. The cafe is filled with patrons. Violinists play their song. New Yorkers stream along the sidewalks. I'm back on my chair—no more tabletop—and with my porcelain coffee mug set firmly before me.

Caelin stands outside once more.

Without so much a glance in my direction, Caelin drops a wad of bills into the couple's fedora and strolls away. I have the insane urge to run after him, yet I manage to stay put.

The memory ends. My heart sinks. Clearly, my hallucinations are back. Another option appears.

People say Caelin is a vampire who wields mind control powers. Maybe that's what happened.

I quickly shove that idiocy aside. *Vampires, really?* Instead of the supernatural, I eye my very real mug of coffee. Stakeouts take forever. I just made a bathroom run and left my drink unattended.

Mystery solved.

There's no mind control magic at work here. Someone drugged my java. I blink hard, wondering if there are any woozy effects still going on. I carefully scan my body and senses.

Nope, I'm fine. I exhale. *What a close call. I'm lucky I just got hit with one short hallucination.*

I try to focus on Ghost's apartment building again. Not happening. All I can do is think about every person I saw over the last six hours. Which one drugged me? And how can I get my revenge? This isn't a helpful activity, so I decide to call it a night. There's plenty of time between now and next Friday.

I'll get the intel for Otto later.

With that thought, a weight of sorrow settles into my bones. I've had my share of ill fortune. But right now? The worst luck I can remember is my minute of fake intimacy with Caelin. It felt so real, and now it's simply another lovely dream that's lost forever. Because girls like me and guys like Caelin?

Impossible.

15

LEXA

*J*hightail it out of the coffee shop. Mom's apartment happens to be close by—*because what isn't near you in Manhattan?*—so I head in that direction. Plus, I need to check on Sash. To be honest, I also need the special kind of reality reinforcement that only my mother can deliver.

I march through one of those neighborhoods that real estate agents label as *in transition*. Fancy marble-covered buildings—like the one Ghost lives in—stand yards away from run-down blocks of concrete where you have to ask: is this a prison or a cheap place to live?

In my family's case, it's the latter. Mom and Sash live in one tiny part of a hulk-sized cinderblock building. Technically, it's my place as well. After all, I pay the rent. It's an efficiency with a main room, galley kitchen, bathroom… and that's it. Living with my family in such a small apartment would be too much togetherness. I stay in my back room 'apartment' at Lucky Ladies.

Soon, I'm opening a heavy wooden door in a skinny passage that's lined with—*surprise, surprise!*—more heavy wooden doors. Even standing on the threshold, I can hear neighbors on either side. On the left wall, there lives an older lady with a potty mouth who loves to scream at the television game shows. Speaking of which, her warbling voice now echoes through the walls.

"Pick a vowel! It's Wheel Of Fortune, not Circle Of Idiots!"

On the right-hand side is a couple who also yell, but only at each other. Again, their voices carry.

"What's this on our credit card? You charged something at the OLLL?" That's the wife.

"I got dinner. Burger and fries." And here's the very sketchy husband.

"Two hundred bucks for burger and fries. You expect me to believe that?"

I wince. OLLL is Otto's Lucky Ladies Lounge. I make a mental note to avoid these neighbors even more than usual.

As I close the door, the scent of stale cigarette smoke hangs in the air. A small hallway winds forward. Mom's voice echoes in from the apartment beyond.

"Lexa, is that you?" asks Mom. "Did you bring my smokes?"

And there it is. The reality I need. No heartfelt hellos, only demands for cigarettes. This is what you call true life. Mom smokes. Neighbors yell. No overly-handsome men in sight.

The place appears as it always does. There's a threadbare rug, tobacco-stained walls, and a pair of pull-out couches that haven't been extended into beds for years. Sash sleeps on one by the window.

My heart melts to see her. My sister's curled onto her side with her back to me. From here, I can see the notches of her spine through the thin blanket.

"Sash?" I ask.

My sister's shoulders rise and fall in a gentle rhythm. Sash has always been able to sleep through anything. It's one of her superpowers.

I find Mom in the galley kitchen. She hangs by the half-open window in sweats, a T-shirt, and her ever-present neckerchief. At one time, my mother was a dark-haired beauty. She could give off such a sultry look, traffic would literally stop. Now, Mom's a wrinkled mess with fake blonde hair and drooping everything. Plus, I know if I sniff her coffee mug, I'll smell vodka.

It would be a funny cliche if it weren't my life.

Mom stubs out a cigarette into an overflowing ashtray. "Smokes, Lexa."

I pull out a pack from my bag and chuck them to her across the kitchen.

Mom catches my toss. "Finally."

I lower my voice to a whisper. "Does Sash look worse to you?"

Mom pulls off the plastic wrapping. "No."

I check out the cabinet where we keep Sash's plasma pens. "Nothing looks different. Do you think they've changed her meds?"

"Nothing that we need to worry about." Mom sets aside her newly-sparked cigarette. "The Gray Woman's always playing around with formulas."

I do a double-take. "The *who* is doing *what?*"

"Doctor Gray at Silver Pharma is known for tweaking formulas on her med trials," says Mom smoothly. "I'm sure it's nothing." She sets the box back into the cabinet. "If you're curious about the pens, you could always ask Otto to pass along a question to Konstantin."

"Otto's not exactly a trustworthy guy."

"Well, Konstantin's the only one who talks directly to Dr. Gray... and Otto is your only contact to Konstantin, so you do the math." Mom looks away. If I didn't know she was unable to experience shame, I'd think she looked guilty just then.

Even though Mom's trying to change the subject, I can't stop thinking about three words: the Gray Woman.

I'm back in the frozen forest. All around me, the tall pines are encased in a thin layer of ice. Sash and I shiver from cold. I clutch a pendant in my hand. A single thought ricochets through my mind. We have to find the Gray Woman.

With all my focus, I will myself back to reality. The frozen woods disappear. I'm back in a smoke-filled kitchen.

Mom narrows her eyes at me. "What happened just now?"

"Nothing."

"Are you having those fucking hallucinations again? We need you sane, honey. This whole shit show is based on you staying not-nuts and paying off your father's debt. You can't fail us now."

One of the keys to dealing with Mom is knowing when to retreat. That would be now.

"Thanks for the pep talk, Mom. See you later."

And I take off and head for home. As far as I'm concerned, this day is officially over.

16

CAELIN

*S*ome friends hunt deer together.

Konstantin and I take down rogue nightlings.

To that end, Konstantin and I hike toward the Cloisters, a castle-style building made of gray stone which sits atop a hill in New York's Washington Heights. It's a medieval art museum. For nightling vampires who started their human life as Viking killers, this place feels rather familiar. They like infesting the Cloisters and causing trouble.

Long story short, this isn't the first time nightlings have infested the museum after hours. One of my bloodkin runs the security staff. We got a call from her about twenty minutes ago.

Konstantin and I march through the small forest surrounding the museum. Moonbeams break through gaps in the trees. If I focus, I catch the far-off roar of car engines. But if I ignore those noises, this place feels like home.

Honestly, I understand why medieval nightling decide to set up shop here. Only, I can't allow them to stay. We can't give humans proof that vampires exist.

For the occasion, I wear black battle leathers and tall boots— it's the same outfit I used to wear during raids in the old days.

Konstantin is wrapped in his traditional Rus furs. For these nightling, the fact that we dress as bloodkin raiders could be enough to make them rethink their decision to occupy the museum. Others need more dramatic convincing.

As we close in on the building, Konstantin and I launch into the same discussion we always have outside this place.

"I'm not cleaning up the mess," says Konstantin. "You've no idea what a pain in the ass it is to get blood off these statues in there."

"You know the rules," I say with a smile. "Whoever made most of the nightling must clean up after themselves."

Only Bloodkin can turn humans into vampires. Konstantin has a bad track record. Mine isn't perfect, either.

Trouble is, humans tend to whine after just a few decades of life. Imagine five hundred years. They track down their makers in revenge—that would be me and Konstantin—and end up hiding out in the Cloisters.

"Even so, you do your share of the killing," says Konstantin. "You can't take part in the fun and not help during clean up."

"Who says I enjoy killing?"

"You're still a raider at heart, even after all these years."

This is Konstantin's classic argument. He's not wrong.

"You should have thought of that before you made our deal."

"That was eight hundred years ago."

"We'll see who made what nightling. It might be my turn."

"It's never your turn," grumbles Konstantin. "This is why I value Lexa so much. It's one the thing I have one over on you."

My blood heats with anger. "Lexa's not a negotiating chip."

Konstantin stops. "Since when do you stand up for humans about anything? I haven't heard you defend them since you were king. Back then, you had bloodkin, humans, and nightling all living together and singing Kumbaya."

I bob my head and consider. "True, but we never sang."

I've been alive for a thousand years. For most of that time, I've been the same cynical man. But, for a few decades long ago, I was a different person. King Caelin. Every so often, my memories dust off and I realize how much King Caelin would loathe Caelin MacGregor.

Konstantin and I pause before the museum's front door. Both of us close our eyes and reach out with our vampire senses. I wield hefty mind control power. Konstantin has some as well. As I stretch my consciousness through the museum, I sense stagnant blood in dead bodies. Bloodkin. I connect with more of my inner vampire power. Beside me, Konstantin does the same.

"Got them?" I ask.

"Da." *Yes.*

When I next speak, I add bloodkin power to my voice. These nightling may not be able to hear me speak, but my words will still echo through their minds.

"This is King Caelin of Clan MacGregor. I'm here with King Konstantin of the Rus. You cannot make a home in the human world. If you step forward and turn yourselves in, we won't kill you. Who wishes to give up?"

A charged silence fills my mind. The bloodkin say *no.*

"Who wishes to fight?" asks Konstantin.

Roars of primal rage fill my mind. I open my eyes and break my mental connection to the bloodkin.

"Foolish choice," I declare.

Beside me, Konstantin takes out obelisk dagger. "They have the right to fight us."

"True." I take out my own pair of obelisk daggers, one for each hand. "If the roles were exchanged, we'd do the same. No warrior wants to die by inches."

Konstantin nods. "Let's go."

In my collection of master keys, I have one for this place from my security contact. I open the front door. A darkened hallway stretches before us. At this point, Konstantin and I could use our powers to connect again to the nightling. We won't, though. That breaks the rules of vampire combat. Just like my wrestling match all those years ago, I must battle these nightling without magic.

Konstantin and I slip through the shadowy passage. It's a gray stone hallway with heavy columns and an arched ceiling. If I were going to attack here, I'd either hide behind a column or lurk in the dark peaks above.

According to vampire rules, using my magic isn't acceptable. But vampire senses are fair game. The barest rustling sounds from over our heads. Konstantin and I lock gazes. He hears the nightling above us, same as I do.

"Are you mine?" asks Konstantin.

No reply.

A smile quirks Konstantin's mouth. "This one's yours. Your people are too proud to answer to anyone else."

A man drops down onto the path before us. He wears rags that were once battle leathers. His dark hair is long and matted. Although his eyes are sunken in, there's no missing how they're a particular shade of bright green. He holds a rusted obelisk dagger in his right hand.

I remember this fellow. Back when I was king, this man asked me to turn him into a vampire so he could be a better warrior. At the time, that was an irresistible request.

"Hello, Graeme."

His mouth twitches. "This is all your fault. I'm not meant to live this long."

I reset one of my obelisk blades into a holster at my hip. If Graeme attacks, I won't need two weapons. "You begged me for immortal life."

"And now, I want death in battle. Will you give that to me as well?"

"Attack me and find out."

I trained this nightling on how to fight, so I fully expect his first move will be a false lunge to the left followed by a real attack from the right.

Graeme doesn't disappoint. When he makes his real assault, I block his strike with one arm while plunging in my obelisk blade with the other. Graeme crumples over.

As he dies, Graeme whispers two words. "Thank you."

What a shame. There's only so much any mind can handle. I should know; I wrestle with the same darkness myself. Kneeling, I brush my fingers over Graeme's face to close his now-unseeing eyes. "Sleep well, my knight."

I look over to Konstantin. He's smiling.

"What has you so happy?" I ask.

"So far, you're cleaning this one up. At last"

I shake my head. Despite the seriousness of the situation, I can't help but smile. Konstantin brims over with passion for life. I reach inside myself, trying to find that same emotion.

Normally, there's nothing.

This time, I do find something. An image. It's Lexa.

Soaking in the image of her fierce eyes and full mouth, power and life thrum through my limbs. It's intoxicating.

It takes an effort, but I somehow set thoughts of Lexa aside. The dead nightling before me is exactly why I must avoid humans like Lexa. It never ends well.

"Let's keep going," I tell Konstantin. "It may be too early to declare victory."

We head into a long and rectangular space whose walls are lined with stone columns. The darkened recesses of the ceiling are shadowy enough to make for good hiding places.

Konstantin and I pause in the center of the room. The air is stale and carries the lingering scents of human tourists. Long seconds pass. Figures step out from behind nearby columns. In short order, I count thirteen nightling before us. Like Graeme, all of them wear their ancient battle leathers.

"Are they yours?" I ask.

"In a way. They're Fyodor's." Konstantin sighs. "I really thought I had you on the cleaning duty for once."

"We'll fight as knights?" I ask.

"Always."

Konstantin and I move to stand back to back. Both of us pull out a second obelisk dagger.

One of the nightling steps forward. She wears a long fur cloak over her leathers. A traditional line of black paint is painted across her face at eye level. She rounds on Konstantin. "Your father made us."

"You're Rus?" I ask.

"We're not Rus. We're Slav." She pulls down the neckline of her leathers, exposing how her neck is covered by overlapping scars of bite marks. "Fyodor made us nightling as punishment. Now we kill his son."

"I killed Fyodor," I state. "There's still time to back down."

"That doesn't matter," says the woman. "You married that monster's daughter." She raises her obelisk dagger high. "Attack!"

Warriors swarm at us. I stab the enemy before me with my right hand. At the same time, I use my left hand to lance a nightling behind me. Konstantin's movements are so fast, he's a blur. Within seconds, twelve of the nightling are down.

One final warrior remains. She races straight for me. As this nightling closes in, I get a better look at my opponent. Something about her seems familiar. My body numbs with shock.

She looks like Lexa.

The nightling rushes toward me with her obelisk dagger high. I tighten my grip on my own weapons. I don't want to kill this nightling, but if she gets too close, I'll be forced.

At the last moment, Konstantin steps between me and the nightling. He slams his obelisk dagger into her heart. The woman crumples over, dead. Konstantin rounds on me.

"What happened?" he asks. There's no need for him to say more. Konstantin wants to know why I didn't attack.

"She reminds me of someone," I state.

Konstantin nods. "Lexa."

"Anything more you wish to tell me?" I ask.

"Nyet." *No.* Konstantin shivers. "And that's the end of it."

Which means Konstantin won't speak about this anymore. I understand. After a thousand years, we both have a long list of things we won't discuss. And I'll get him to tell at a later time, probably over more whiskey.

Konstantin cracks his neck. "I'll summon my crew for clean up."

"And I'll get mine as well." There's no question why, either. I add the reason aloud.

"Fyodor is a legacy and liability for both of us."

17

LEXA

*W*here is Ghost?

For days, I've waited for the guy to show up. It's getting annoying. If I were sloppy, I'd just have Otto's guys break in. But there are three big problems with that. One, I don't know how to open the safe. Two, I can't confirm what's inside the safe. And three, no matter how much a target is away from home, they show up the second someone's going through their stuff.

I try to kill time looking into Ghost's background, but the guy keeps a clean profile. I don't even know what he looks like.

After another eight hours of sitting on my ass and staring out a window, I call it quits.

Time for home sweet home.

Or in my case, strip club sweet strip club.

After a few train and bus rides, I'm marching toward the Lucky Ladies Lounge. It's a small brick building on a street of empty warehouses. Inside, the place is seedy and dank. A patchwork of small round tables surrounds a raised platform. This time of day, there are a few hard drinkers in the audience and no talent performing.

I head to the back wall marked, *offices*. This empties out onto a thin wooden hallway. The first door on my left is Otto's place. Toward the end of the passage, that's the utility closet that serves as my bedroom.

After taking in a few deep breaths, I knock on the door. "Otto?"

"Yeah,"

I open the door and step inside. The place is a seedy little room with a single chair, cramped desk, and piles of paper everywhere. Pictures of naked women hang on the walls. An open bottle of bourbon waits atop a nearby filing cabinet.

Otto lounges behind his desk. His round face is covered in a thin sheen of sweat. He wears a wife-beater shirt and several gold chains.

"You've got my fucking report?" asks Otto.

"No, I told you. I'll have it by next Friday."

"Then why the fuck are you in my office?"

"We need to talk about Ghost. The guy isn't showing up at his apartment. Can you get me more intel? All I have is an address. This isn't enough."

"Work with what you got." Otto belches. "Which makes me wonder... what the fuck are you doing here? Shouldn't you be back at that coffee shop and watching Ghost's apartment? Don't whine at me when you aren't doing your job."

"Thanks for the support, Otto. You're a great help."

Otto leans back on his chair and kicks his legs onto the desktop. "Go bitch at someone who cares, Lexa."

Rage careens through my body. After all the years of working together, how can Otto be such a dick?

Stay calm, Lexa. Getting angry at Otto is like yelling at the wind.

Leaving my crap boss, I march along the dark corridor behind the club's back wall. It's a short walk until I reach the door to my room. Although, to use the term *door* is being generous. It's more of a thin wooden plank that covers the small utility closet where I sleep. *My so-called apartment.* It's not the Ritz, but it's secure and free. In New York, that means something.

After sliding the wooden plank aside, I step into what serves as my bedroom. It's a small square made of cinderblock. The many shelves hold cleaning supplies. A lonely mop sits in a roller bucket. My bed's a camping cot that leans against the far wall. My drawing supplies, clothes, and satchel are all stowed under the bed.

For the first time in ages, I reach under the cot and pull out my old notebook and a tin of drawing pencils. It seems like a million years ago that I last sketched my sister Sash for Legacy Day at Paxton High.

I start drawing in broad strokes. I've nothing in particular in mind, but an image quickly appears.

Caelin MacGregor.

Once I realize what I'm creating, I reset my stuff under the bed. *Forget drawing.* After changing into a T-Shirt and boy shorts, I try to get some rest.

It isn't easy.

To begin with, it takes forever for me to fall asleep. When I do conk out, I dream I'm inside Ghost's apartment. I open the walk-in safe inside his bedroom wall. Inside, I find someone I didn't expect.

"Mom?"

My mother gestures across her throat. Normally, she wears tons of makeup to hide the scars on her throat. Now, her skin is bare. And for the first time in what feels like ever, I can see how her neck is covered in bite marks. Even more strange, the scars look as if they're made from fangs.

"You don't know who I am," says Mom.

"Who bit you?"

"Vampires."

I shake my head in disbelief. "Those don't exist."

"*You* don't exist, honey."

Bam! Bam!

Loud knocks sound on my door, jarring me out of sleep.

"Wake up!" It's Otto.

I open my eyes, finding myself back in my bedroom. Exhaling, I lean my head back onto the pillow.

That was all a dream. Good.

Otto slams on my door again. "Move your ass, Lexa!"

"What do you want?"

"Put on a bikini. I've got a contest and nothing but dogs."

"Women are not dogs," I point out. "Besides, I spent all day casing out Vice. I need some rest."

Otto pushes the door aside. He stands on the threshold to my little room. "I said, I've got a bikini contest and no tits. You're up."

"No."

"Turn on your gift."

"I call it my curse." It's also the secret to the best of my surveillance. I wear boxy clothes and repeat Mom's old mantra.

Act submissive.
Don't make eye contact.
Be invisible.

And it works. Most days, I live my life that way. Still, there are times when I turn on the charm, like the Bikini contest. The clientele here are just like Otto. All they need are big breasts and a smile.

If Sash were here, she'd say something about how vampires inspire three reactions from humans: fear, desire, and nothing. But Sash is out of touch with reality. I work in a strip club. My superpower for grabbing attention isn't latent vampire skills, it's my large breasts.

Thinking about Sash makes another memory knock around

the back of my head. Did I dream about vampires last night? No matter how much I try, I can't recall a thing now.

Otto steps into my little space. There's no desire in his gaze. If anything, Otto stares at me the way I look at Sash's plasma pen. A useful possession.

"Come on, Lexa. Who keeps you safe from Konstantin? Who puts a roof over your head?"

I sit up and roll my eyes. "You're a saint."

Otto lowers his voice. "Who makes sure sad little Sasha has her meds?"

And that's always the one that gets me.

"Fine. I'll do it."

18

LEXA

*B*ikini contest, here I come. Yay.

I've called the Lucky Ladies home for years. In all that time, I've become buddies with some performers. Many say they come alive when stepping onstage. Not gonna lie. I envy that. Because, when I walk into the spotlight, it's like my toe got stuck in a light socket. All I want to do is run.

Even so, the sooner I get started, the faster my time on stage will end. I change into a bikini and flip-flops. Although my little pink swimsuit has never touched the ocean, it's still gotten frayed up top. My breasts have grown over the years, but not my wallet. That's a sad fact, right there.

As I step out of my room, I grab my favorite robe. It's a long silk number that I tie at the waist. Now covered, I slog my way down the access corridor and into the club itself. And maybe I feel a little sorry for myself.

This is no time for a self-pity party. Rally, Lexa.

Straightening my spine, I step into the club proper. Like always, the place smells like old sneakers. A patchwork of small round tables sit before a raised platform. A line of two women stands by the stage. Both wear bikinis.

I cross the room, ready to take my place in the line of contestants. As I step along, a chill crawls up my neck.

Someone watches me.

Pausing, I scan the crowd, but the faces are all uniformly unfamiliar. My mind must be playing tricks on me. I just woke up, after all.

I take my place in line. Up close, I can get a better look at the other contestants. One is fit, petite, and lean. She's the type who runs triathlons for fun. Blonde hair, blue bikini, and—in my opinion—a total winner.

The second is dark skinned, tall, and lithe. She should be on a runway in couture, not hanging out in Otto's place. I know some agents make their models do the contest circuit for exposure. Coming here is a mistake such ladies only make once.

In my opinion, these women are far better looking than I am. Plus, they're smiley and wearing make-up. Neither has bed head, a fact that is not true in my case.

I'm more chesty. That's it.

Otto's such a pig.

Think of Sash. Get this over with.

Otto spots me as I move through the crowd. Although he wears a smile, there's no missing the muscle that twitches along Otto's neck. He's angry that I'm late.

Oh, well. He'll recover.

As I take my place as the last in line, the crowd launches into a rowdy drunken chant.

"We want the show! We want the show!"

Otto slams the microphone against his palm. A combination thud and mechanical squeak slices through the smoky air. That shuts the audience up and how.

"Welcome to the Lucky Ladies Amateur Night Bikini Contest!" calls Otto. "I'm about to bring three random local beauties onto the stage. Whoever gets the most cheers wins not one, but two hundred dollars! Let's check out contestant number three!"

The athlete steps up onstage. The crowd applauds.

"Now, contestant number two!"

The model struts into the spotlight. More cheers.

"And now, our last contestant." Otto gestures toward me. "Get up here, number one!"

I take my place in line. That's when I realize I never took off my robe. And I really don't want to.

"Don't be shy," says Otto. "Let's see that bikini."

I pull the tie loose and slip off my robe. Once again, it's time for mom's classic advice.

> *Act submissive.*
> *Don't make eye contact.*
> *Be invisible.*

Sure enough, no one looks. I don't even get a clap. It's pretty satisfying.

Otto elbows me. "Smile, Lexa."

Much as I enjoy ruining Otto's night, it's not like I can keep this up forever. I've been in this situation before. Otto's not ending things until I grin and pose. So, that's what I do. It helps to repeat something different in my mind.

> *See me. Want me.*

All eyes seem to focus in my direction. Waves of hunger and desire roll off the audience in waves. Everyone cheers. My insides churn with revulsion. This part is nothing new. What's different are the thoughts running through my head.

> *This is wrong. I'm predator, not prey.*

The realization is so unexpected, I lose track of time. Since when do I see the world in terms of predator and prey? I'm vaguely aware of Otto raising his hand over the head of contestant number three. The crowd claps. Otto moves on to contestant number two. More applause.

When my mind clears, I realize Otto's raised his hand above my head. "Who likes contestant number one?"

For whatever reason, the crowd loses their collective sanity. Guess Otto isn't the only breast lover in the city.

"And the winner of a cool two hundred in prize money is contestant number one, Lexa!"

While the audience keeps roaring their approval, I turn to Otto and hold out my hand. If I don't do this, Otto 'forgets' to pay me. My boss slams a pile of cash onto my palm.

"That's light," I say, because it is. "You owe my fifty more dollars."

Otto adds more bills and stomps offstage.

I exhale. *It's over.*

Slipping on my robe, I head back to my room and try to fall asleep. For a while, I stay awake and try to recapture my dreams from last night. It was something about vampires. Although I can't remember what happened, I still want that dream again.

With that thought, I finally drift off to sleep.

19

LEXA

*G*host, *you're officially a pain in my ass.*

All the days blur together as I spend them all at the same table, waiting for my target to show up.

In the meantime, I've become an expert on Big Apple Coffee. So far, I've learned when to hit the bathroom (first thing in the morning)... how to order the best bagel (request H&H, they keep the crap stuff for tourists)... and most of all, I know who needs their ass kissed, early and often (that would be Penny, the store manager).

Once again, I've scored my favorite table by the window. The lunch rush is over. Penny stops by, coffee pot in hand.

"Want a refill?" she asks.

"Yes, thanks." I slap a twenty-dollar bill on the table. "Keep the change."

Penny picks up the cash. "How's it going with the evil ex?"

I needed a story about why I parked here all day long, other than a desire to leave good tips. Penny thinks my ex-husband lives in the apartment across the street, and the cheater is trying to screw me out of a decent divorce settlement. I'm gathering evidence.

I hold up my phone. "I almost got a pic of Leonard's floozy yesterday."

Penny nods. "We're all pulling for you."

I can't help but smile. Even in New York City, the wait-staff gossip. No one questions why I can't afford a private investigator, yet I can shell out massive tips. That's human nature for you.

Penny steps onto the next table. I lean back on my chair and wait for Mister Elusive to show up.

Any time now, Ghost.

There has been one development in my surveillance. Lately, every time I start my stakeout, there's a sign that Ghost just left the apartment, such as fresh dishes in the sink or a rumpled bed. This man is slippery.

That ends today. I've decided to just park my ass until Ghost shows up. I'm now on hour thirty-two and my ass cheeks are numb. Still, there's no way I'm giving up now.

More hours pass. Eventually, the violinists show up. Tunes help to pass the time. Every so often, the artists hand out postcards for their Friday night performances at House of Music. I'm so sleepy, the thought that I'll never go to a dressy place like that doesn't even depress me.

At some point, I crack out a paper notebook and start sketching a random man in a tuxedo with piercing eyes, broad shoulders, and a very kissable mouth.

On second thought, the guy looks a lot like Caelin.

I tear up the Caelin pic into little pieces. I've waited here too long to get distracted now. Besides, that wasn't the real Caelin MacGregor. That was just a drug-induced joke.

At last, a light flickers on in Ghost's second-story window. My pulse speeds. That said, I try not to get too excited. Ghost's building is one of those fancy places with maid service. Just because a light goes on, that doesn't mean my target is home.

Across the street, a man becomes visible through Ghost's

living room window. It's definitely not a maid. Every nerve ending in my body goes on alert.

I know this guy. He may go by the code name Ghost, but it's actually a douchebag from high school.

Vice.

There's no missing that pointy chin, over-large eyes, and spiked-up hair. Back in high school, Vice was a scrawny kid with knobby knees and a massive Adam's apple. Now, the guy is jacked. Even more tattoos cover his neck and face.

An electric charge of shock careens through my nervous system. Vice is in the city and running jobs? It's more than possible. Vice's alter ego, Ghost, is a well-known freelancer.

Over in the apartment, Vice steps into his bedroom and pulls aside a drape that covers the wall across from the window. My breath catches.

There it is. The walk-in safe.

It's on old-school model with a massive dial. Vice spins in the combination. I make note of the movements. Even without him opening the thing in front of me, I could crack this safe, no problem.

The metal door swings open. Based on my intel, this safe should be filled with gold bars. When it comes to a heist, there really is nothing better.

Stacks of gold glimmer within the safe. So far, so good. But, there's also the image of a woman pasted to the inside of the safe's door.

It could be me.

My eyes widen with shock. Before, I thought it was just coincidence that Ghost—I mean, Vice—kept skipping out right before I got into my surveillance spot. But what if I've been his target this whole time? Everyone knows Konstantin has a top earner who does stakeouts for the Bratva. If Vice knows I'm that person, then everyone who hates Konstantin can just kidnap or kill me for revenge.

And Konstantin has a lot of enemies.

Even worse, the top person I suspect may want to do me harm is Vice himself. I need to get in and see. Is that really my picture in his safe?

Suddenly, it's even more important to understand Vice's schedule. There's no way I'm stepping into that apartment unless I know Vice is somewhere else.

How can I get an idea of where Vice will be and when?

Rising, I grab my satchel and speed out of the coffee shop. Otto must know something useful about Vice, even if my boss doesn't realize that he has the information.

I'm heading for the Lucky Ladies.

Time to confront Otto and get some useful intel.

20

CAELIN

8:13 pm.

I sit in my inner office, watching the wall of monitors flicker through different scenes from my properties. There are entrances. Back alleys. Rooftops. This late in the day, there are few humans around. For some reason, it's comforting to watch this emptiness.

One monitor stays locked on the entrance to the Nouveau Palais. I scan through last night's footage. Using the control panel on my desktop, I speed through the video of New Yorkers coming and going.

After my strange encounter with Lexa, I did some digging. Konstantin has Lexa staking out the Nouveau Palais. A freelance killer named ghost lives in the building, along with his collection of gold bars.

I watch onscreen as yet another human walks across the lobby of the Nouveau Palais. My senses go on alert Something about this man feels familiar. I pause the video feed and press a few buttons. The image expands until I can see the man's face. My brows lift with surprise.

It's Vice, Prudence's brother.

As in, this is the kid I moved to New York. Now, he's living in one of my buildings under an assumed name. Using the security cameras, I track Vice to his apartment.

Turns out, Vice is actually Ghost, the highest paid assassin in New York. And Lexa is watching his apartment.

My mouth thins to a determined line. Protective energy rises within me. Konstantin shouldn't place his people at risk in this way. Some small part of me points out that I never got upset about such things before. Is it that I don't like Konstantin placing his people at risk... or that I don't want Lexa in the line of fire?

A knock sounds on the door. I press a button. The wall of monitors goes dark.

"Come in," I state.

Prudence enters. She looks as prim and buttoned-up as ever. "Good morning, sir."

"Prudence, it's far too early. You shouldn't be here at this hour."

"I can't. There's simply too much work to do."

I tilt my head. "And one of those tasks should be finding me a personal assistant."

"Of course."

Prudence and I are still playing this game. I ask for a personal assistant. Prudence pretends to look for one.

"Have a seat." I gesture to the open chair across from my desk.

"Oh, I'm far too busy."

"Sit down anyway." Prudence quickly takes her chair. "You know I have powers of mind control. I'll give you a chance to answer a question freely. Let's talk about your brother, Vice."

"Oh, he's fine. We're so thankful you moved him to the city years ago. He works at a garage in uptown. Vice is quite the mechanic."

"Ah." I lean forward in my chair. "Any reason why Konstantin would be interested in your brother?"

Prudence's gaze locks on my desk. Or rather, a particular item on it. I recently moved a few personal things to my inner office, including an obelisk dagger that once belonged to Konstantin's father, Fyodor. The weapon sits under a small glass case on my desktop. Prudence can't keep her eyes off it.

I take the blade out from under its glass covering. "Would you like to hold it?"

"Yes, please," says Prudence quickly.

I hand the weapon over. Prudence reverently brushes her fingers along the weapon. Intricate runes are carved onto the handle.

"Do you have any idea who owned that dagger?"

"Fyodor the Rus," answers Prudence. Her eyes widen as she realizes her mistake. Modern scholars don't even know Fyodor the Rus ever existed. Prudence quickly resets the item onto the desktop. "Or, that's what Hunter told me."

And that's something else to discuss with Hunter when he arrives tomorrow morning.

"I'll ask again. What is Vice doing?"

Prudence clasps her hands tightly in her lap. "I lied before. My brother has become an assassin for hire. I haven't spoken to him in years."

When I next speak, I tap into Prudence's heartbeat. Her pulse sounds in my head as I press vampire magic into my voice. "He's really Ghost—is that the truth?"

"Aye. I mean, yes."

"Glad to hear it." I keep the magic in my voice as I ask another question. "Who's Ghost working for these days?"

"Himself, I guess. I really don't know."

I drum my fingers on the desktop. That was another true answer. Still, instinct tells me Prudence is scheming. And if she's an admirer of Fyodor the Rus, then I'm her least favorite person. After all, I killed the man.

I shake my head. How can I suspect Prudence? She's human.

There's no way she can know the truth about Fyodor. Besides, if Prudence wanted me dead, why wait so long to attack?

Perhaps it's time to inspect one of my properties more closely. Vice's apartment in the Nouveau Palais may yield interesting results. In the meantime, it's best to keep my potential enemy close. I force my face into a mask of calm.

"You came in here for a reason, Prudence?"

"Your soeur, Kiki, is here. It's time for her donation."

Soeurs are another name for blood sisters. In my case, they are all women and more than fairly compensated for their services. And I watch each one carefully for signs of red madness. Once a soeur gets too possessive, I pay them well and send them away.

"She's in your central meeting room now," adds Prudence.

"Send her in."

Prudence steps away and Kiki enters my inner office. She's tall and pale with an oval face, piercing dark eyes, and a full mouth. Her blue kimono wraps loosely around her. I scan her for any signs of red madness. She's fine.

Kiki steps around in a slow circle. "We never meet in here."

"First time for everything."

Kiki allows her kimono to fall to her shoulders. She tilts her head, offering her throat.

I step up, pausing just before her. I scent the blood pulsing in her veins. My fangs throb as they descend. I gently set my palms on the bare skin of Kiki's shoulders. I lean in and bite.

A surge of blood fills my mouth. Kiki is one of the soeurs where our relationship can get physical. As I take in more blood, my desire rises. Kiki runs her hand down my hardening length.

And for a time, the emptiness within me fades.

21

LEXA

The next morning, I pace a line in front of Mom and Sash's apartment building. My throat tightens with worry. No question about it. This situation with Vice is fraying my nerves.

For years, I've lived by one rule: always deliver for Otto and Konstantin. Sure, I could set up operations, fast and dirty. But, there's a reason I'm the best—I look into every detail and contingency. Nothing goes wrong because my stuff is bulletproof.

And if I research whether Vice is following me, I could miss my deadline for the safe. That might mean no more meds for Sash. Yet, if I don't dig more deeply, then I might be opening myself up to being attacked.

Either way, my sister could end up hurt.

Whatever happens next, Sash should have a say.

I straighten my spine and firm up my resolve. As I step up to the building, a chill crawls up my neck.

Someone's watching me.

Pausing, I scan my surroundings. The street looks like it always does. It's the same mangy trees, blocky buildings, and oblivious pedestrians.

At some point, I realize I've been standing in the same spot for way too long. If someone's watching, they're well hidden. Plus, I had a crap night's sleep. My sleep-deprived brain may be playing tricks on me.

I march inside the building until I reach Mom and Sash's door. Something unexpected dangling from the handle: a white plastic bag that reads *'prescription delivery.'*

Which is strange.

Sash's meds are dropped with all the falderal of a gold delivery to Fort Knox. An old guy, Wayne, drops off the meds in a plain paper bag. Mom has to sign for the shipment and keep a copy of the receipt. All that takes place in the mailroom. Wayne never steps inside the building.

Delivery folks don't sashay into the building and leave thirty-five thousand dollars worth of plasma pens on a doorknob.

I grab the bag and navigate the long line of keys and locks that are standard in New York. After opening the door, I find a post-card sitting on the floor. It's the same color as the postcard the violinists hand out. Since Big Apple Coffee is around the corner, I figure my favorite street musicians are trying to drum up some excitement for their Friday nights at the House of Music.

Still, how did they get in here, too? Worry and rage churn inside me. I pay good money for this apartment, even if I don't use it. The least the landlords can do is keep the front door locked.

I step inside the access hallway. "Mom? Sash?"

No response.

I enter the main room to find Sash asleep on the couch. I check the kitchen, but the lack of cigarette smoke already told me the truth. Mom's not here.

Sash yawns. "Afternoon, Lexa."

"Hey, sis." I open a kitchen cabinet and start putting away the new meds from the bag. "Do you need a pen?"

"Yes, please."

I leave one box in the bag and hand the whole thing over to Sash. Sadly, my sister has never looked more pale or thin. Sash digs through the bag, pulls out a plasma pen, and jams it under her pillow.

"I keep one here in case of emergencies," she explains. Sash turns over the postcard. "Did you see this?"

My sister can get unreasonably excited about things like dance nights at dressy clubs where we'll never go. "We have more important stuff to talk about first. Where's Mom?"

Sash yawns again. "Gone."

"I thought Mom was always with you. That's why I work while she smokes Marlboro reds."

"Nah. Mom's got a secret life. I let her have it." Sash says that so sweetly, I almost feel guilty for pointing out that Mom even leaves the apartment.

Almost, but not quite.

I point to the front door. "Another thing. Who leaves expensive medication on a door handle?"

A little crinkle appears between Sash's eyebrows. "What happened to Wayne?"

"That's my question, exactly."

"I don't know who leaves the meds. I'm always asleep."

"And this is why Mom shouldn't take off without telling anyone. What if someone stole your meds?"

"It's a good question. Thank you for caring." Sash's smile turns even sweeter, if that were possible. "Can we get back to the postcard?"

"You're aggressively nice, you know that?"

"It's a skill. Look at this postcard already."

I plunk onto the floor, lying down so I'm parallel to Sash, only on the carpet instead of the couch. Cleanness-wise, there isn't much difference.

"Hold on, Sash. I need your advice first." My tone clearly adds, *and it's important.*

"Of course." Sash leans back so we're both staring at the same stretch of moldy ceiling.

"I'm working a new surveillance gig," I begin. "It's supposed to be a safe full of money inside the apartment of a criminal named Ghost." I push my lips together, trying not to reveal the truth. That doesn't last very long. "Ghost is really Vice."

"Oh, that's good."

"Good? I'm talking about Viceroy, our arch-nemesis from high school."

"We were all kids back then. Maybe he's a good man now."

I look up from my spot. "Are you serious?" Sash looks as sweet and genuine as always. I sigh. "You're serious."

"What's wrong with staking out Vice's apartment?" asks Sash. "That's what you do."

"Ghost's safe may have a picture of me inside it. Which means he could be watching me. And if it's discovered that I'm Konstantin's top earner, my life gets tricky."

"You could always tell Konstantin. He might help."

"Are you serious again?" I ask.

"I've never met Konstantin. He could be kind."

"You're too sweet, you know that?"

She chuckles. "It's a skill."

"I should look into all this." I sigh. " But that would mean going beyond what I usually do, which will take way more time. I'm starting from zero on Vice. I could miss my deadline for Otto and that might affect you, too. I'm stuck."

"You have until next Friday," says Sash. "There's lots of time left."

"If I fail, that could mean the end of your meds. So, if I keep looking into this, I need you to understand the risk."

"Ah. You want my call?"

"Please."

Sash folds her hands neatly on her chest. "Do your own

research on Vice. Don't worry about Konstantin. You drive enough money for the man. You can rattle his cage."

I shake my head. "Wow. You look so nice but there's steel in there."

Sash rolls over onto her side so she can look down at me. "Lexa, you must track this down. It's what you're born to do." She switches onto her back again. "That and draw pictures."

"Thanks." I take in a deep breath. "You're right, I need to find out what's happening." I press my palms against my eyes. "Only question is, how?"

Normally, this is the kind of thing I love to do. Maybe it's because I'm still freaked out about the hallucination with Caelin MacGregor, but I'm still having trouble focusing. Not that I tell Sash anything. She doesn't need to know my hallucinations are back.

"Now, can I talk about the postcard?" asks Sash.

"Yes, sure."

"It's about Empire Investments. They're hiring."

"Come on. What does it say?"

"I'm serious." Sash hands over the postcard. Sure enough, it's in the same color as the one from the House of Music, but it says something very different. "Wow, they're hiring. I did not see this coming."

"I know! This postcard is about a personal assistant job for the richest man alive. Talk about karma."

It strikes me as odd that someone might have delivered the meds and postcard together, but any questions about that get snowed under another, bigger query. "How does this help me, exactly?"

"Everyone knows Caelin's involved with the underworld," answers Sash. "Caelin might know if Vice is following you and why. Personal assistants get access to everything."

"Getting hired might take a while."

"Or you might find out everything you need during the interview. You're irresistible when you want to be."

"That is, *if* I get the interview."

"You could also try for a job at Silver Pharma."

"I tried that before; Silver is locked down tight. There are a million background checks just to get a job interview. I failed them all, fast. But Empire Investments? I hadn't thought of that before."

"I can tell the idea appeals," says Sash. "Admit it. You have a crush on Caelin MacGregor."

I roll my eyes. "Sash."

"Everyone says Caelin might be a vampire," adds Sash.

"Vampires don't exist!"

Not for the first time, I realize I'm way too passionate about the topic of vampires. A memory itches at the back of my mind. I shove it aside.

When Sash next speaks, her voice carries a dreamy tone. "Sometimes, when I'm really sick, I see you and I climbing up a mountain. We're hiding from vampires and visiting a water elemental. Does that sound crazy?"

I hop to my feet. "Why would you say something like that? It doesn't make any sense."

Sash sighs. "You're right. It doesn't."

A weight of guilt settles onto my shoulders. How could I snap at someone as sweet as Sash? I sit on the edge of the couch. "Hey, we don't remember life from when we were kids. It's natural to want to fill in the blanks."

Sash nods. "If you want to work out your guilty conscience, you can get my laptop. It's under the couch."

"Am I that obvious?"

"To me?" Sash winks. "Always."

I pull out the laptop and type in web address from the postcard. A page from Empire Investments appears. "It's a really short form," I report. "Just my name and address." I enter the required info and nibble my lower lip. "Should I do it?"

"Yes!" Sash goes into a coughing fit.

I get her some water and return my attention to the laptop. I double-check everything and hit *send.*

This shouldn't make me so excited.

Yet, it does.

22

CAELIN

5:59 a.m.

Any minute now, Hunter will meet my deadline and land his plane in New York. I await him on the tarmac. This is one benefit of owning your own landing strip and hangar. No security hassles.

The sky lightens with the first signs of dawn. Mine is a small airport: just a single runway. A wide field surrounds the asphalt. Beyond the low grasses, lines of identical houses stretch off to the horizon. Human suburbia.

I remember when this spot was nothing but old forest and Iroquois territory. Back then, I marched under the trees along with Hunter and Indigo. Now it's all planes, runways, and suburbia. Some days, it doesn't seem real.

A small dark spot appears in the cloudy sky. The shape grows until it becomes a mini jet. As the plane flies overhead, the engines roar. Heated wind whips past me.

Hunter touches down so the plane's landing gear stops within inches of my chest. *His idea of humor.* Hunter hops out the plane's side door, landing right beside me. "You're on the tarmac."

"It's good business practice to inspect your possessions." I scan the asphalt from left to right. "Looks fine."

"That's not what I mean. This is more than inspecting some little airport on your balance sheet." He sets his fists on his hips. "You've got a twinkle in your eyes."

"I don't twinkle. Ever."

"Ah, let me guess. I'm here because of Prudence. She called me yesterday."

"Seriously?"

Hunter nods. "According to Prudence, she needs to get enhanced. The Gray Woman—I mean, Silver Pharma—won't do it for her. Prudence thinks I can put in a good word."

"And can you?"

"I'll put in a word, but it's not good. I don't trust Prudence."

"I only trust her to lie. She asked me if I could help her get enhanced years ago. I refused. Interesting that she's bringing it back up again now. And to you, no less. By the way, have you ever mentioned Fyodor the Rus to her?"

"Are you serious? I haven't mentioned that bastard's name since you jammed an obelisk dagger through his heart."

"Prudence mentioned him yesterday. She says *you* gave her the name."

Hunter stares at me for a long moment. "You want me to check on Prudence?"

"Is your network up to it?"

"All my best informants are still alive. Anything else?"

"Check into Prudence's brother, Vice. He now goes by the name Ghost and styles himself as an assassin."

"Will do."

"Oh, and if you see notice a human woman following Vice, do not engage."

"A woman?" Hunter grins. "Your twinkling eyes are starting to make more sense now."

"It's not what you think. Lexa may have been enhanced with the powers of a mindlock daemon. She causes hallucinations."

"Or, it could be something else, though," says Hunter. "The Gray Woman might have enhanced her into a female bloodkin." I hear the note of expectation in his voice. There's no question where he's going with this.

Fated mates.

How I hate to crush his hope. Still, there's no point believing in lies.

"It's not fated mates," I say carefully. "That's not possible."

"Anything else?"

"Don't mention anything about this to Konstantin," I state. "The woman who's following Vice is Lexa Uznetsov. She's Konstantin's earner."

A long pause follows before Hunter speaks again. "Damn. If he thinks we're going after his rainmaker, he'll kill us."

"Don't worry about Konstantin," I state. "Whatever happens, I can handle him."

Hunter chuckles. "When King Caelin fights, we can't lose."

I turn Hunter's words over in my mind. *When King Caelin fights.* Over the last centuries, I've only indulged in rage or grief. But the urge to fight and protect?

I'd almost forgotten how good it felt.

23

CAELIN

*T*he next morning, I wake up to a cryptic text message from Hunter. He's waiting for me to pick him up in front of Empire Investments.

Which means Hunter already has results on his reconnaissance work. That's fast, even for him.

Minutes later, I drive my Porsche toward the entrance to my headquarters. Hunter is there, wearing cargo pants, a black T-shirt, and hefty boots. There's no missing the dark circles under his eyes. The man hasn't slept since he landed yesterday.

And if my hunch is right, Hunter has some good information for me.

I pull up onto the curb, careful to stop inches away from Hunter. At the same time, I reach out with my vampire senses. I can feel the blood pumping in nearby humans. I connect to their collective life force and send a message.

I'm not here.

There are a lot of humans around, so the pull on my inner energy is strong. It's also worth it. The humans keep marching, oblivious to the fact that I've decided to park on the sidewalk.

Hunter slides into the passenger seat and slams the door. "Nice payback."

I can't help but smile. "I'm king. I can't ignore when my second in command almost runs me over with his airplane."

"It's *your* plane," corrects Hunter. "I'm just a servant."

"And where does my servant wish to go?"

"I checked all my best contacts. The vampire coven, Brooklyn nightling, even some human hackers. Based on their intel, we need to interrogate someone right now."

"Address?"

"Forget it. I know your system. I want to be dropped off. And if I give you an address, you'll slip out and leave me to drive. This is my lead."

"But I'm the one with superior powers of mind control."

Hunter sniffs. "Make a right at the light."

I make the turn. "What have you learned?"

"Word is, Vice is working on his own. He has some kind of vendetta against Lexa."

"His sister talked about Fyodor the Rus," I state.

"Not sure how that would ever connect to Lexa. More likely, Vice has a score to settle with Konstantin—and he's already been enhanced by the Gray Woman."

"What powers?"

"Vampire stealth. I've run across other guys with that injection. It might help a bit with humans, but on bloodkin? Nothing." Hunter gestures toward the windshield. "Make your next left."

With that turn, I know exactly where we're going. Lexa's apartment building. As we close in on the spot, I pull the Porsche over, pop it in park, and slip out.

"Not again," groans Hunter. "How did you know?"

I stand with my left arm braced on the open door. "You're not the only one who does research," I reply. "Once I saw we were heading here, I figured he's staking out Lexa's building."

"You sneaky bastard," deadpans Hunter.

"Your Sneaky Majesty Bastard," I correct. Hunter closes the door and speeds away.

Here we go.

I stroll along the sidewalk. This street holds rows of identical concrete towers separated by narrow alleys. Lexa's building is located up ahead and across the street. As I walk along, I scan the alleys. Sure enough, someone lurks in the one directly across from what's listed as Lexa's home.

I step into the darkened passage. A figure hides in the shadows. The moment I enter the alley, the stranger starts to leave. I connect to his inner energy and issue an unspoken demand. *Stay.*

The man stops moving.

I step deeper into the darkness. The person in the shadows becomes clear. Sure enough, it's Vice.

"Ca... Ca... Caelin MacGregor. Is that you?"

"Aye. And you're Viceroy Alekhin, the boy I saved and sent to New York. How disappointing to find you lurking in an alley."

"I'm not here to hurt you," says Vice. "This is about me and Konstantin. The man is trying to steal my gold so I'm tracking his earner. When I hurt her, I hurt Konstantin."

My logical side says that Vice isn't telling me the whole truth. This anger about Konstantin is about more than a safe stuffed with gold bars. That insight is quickly buried under an avalanche of rage.

How dare Vice target Lexa?

I stalk closer, pausing a few feet away. Vice plasters himself against the wall and tries to slip past me.

"That won't work," I state. "Whatever stealth powers you've been enhanced with, they mean nothing to bloodkin."

Vice freezes in place. "Don't kill me."

"Give me one good reason not to."

Vice shows wrist with figure eight infinity on it. "Dr. Gray wouldn't like it."

And she's not the only one. Prudence is still in my employ.

She has access to some of my best secrets. If I want to get rid of Vice, I need to plan it carefully.

"Leave Lexa alone," I declare. "Or else, I will end you."

"Yes, your Majesty."

"Go," I order. Vice runs off into the shadows.

As I watch Vice race away, I consider my next move. The time has come to pay a visit to the Gray Woman. Whatever is happening, she's behind it all.

My phone vibrates in my pocket. I pick it up. It's Prudence. She doesn't wait for any greetings.

"You must forgive my brother," says Prudence. Her voice is high-pitched and laced with worry. "This is my fault. I told Vice that it doesn't matter who he stalks, so long as someone's paying."

I know a lie when I hear it. And that's a big one.

"I thought you two weren't speaking," I state.

"After you brought up Vice, I got worried and reached out to him. This is all my fault. Please don't hurt him."

"He's fine." *For now.*

I end the call.

Hunter pulls up to the alley's mouth. I slip into the Porsche and relate how Vice is after Konstantin. I keep the Lexa part to myself.

"You know what this means," I begin.

"A visit to Silver Pharma," finishes Hunter. "I am not getting near that crazy elemental."

"That won't be a problem." I add one final thought.

"I can handle the Gray Woman alone."

24

LEXA

*T*his is like one of those movies where I keep having the same day, over and over. Only in my case, my day is spent sitting Big Apple Coffee while watching Vice's apartment. I still need to get in there and confirm whether Vice has a picture of me.

Trouble is, Vice is now hanging out in his apartment 24/7. In the surveillance business, we have a name for guys like Vice.

Nightmare target.

Vice keeps the blinds drawn low. All I can see is his shadow moving around, but I know he's there.

There's nothing to do but wait. I can't sneak into a place unless I know I've got a solid stretch of time to look around. After all, this man's an assassin.

I yawn. Spots appear before my eyes. Clearly, I've been watching this man for too long. Maybe Vice doesn't need any sleep, but I have my limits. If I keep this up, I'll start hallucinating again.

Lucky Ladies, here I come.

I step away from my favorite table at the big apple, careful to leave a good tip. The musicians are outside. They know me now, just like the coffee shop staff. As I step past, the two perk up.

"Any luck with the ex-husband?" asks the old man.

"Oh, yeah." I toss some cash into their collective hat. "I'll nail his ass soon."

"Good," says the elder woman. "When you find a new beaux, come dancing at the House of Music."

I can't help but chuckle. *New beaux? In reality, I've never had an old beaux, let alone a replacement.*

The man hands me one of their postcards. "Don't forget us!"

I wink. "That's not possible." I turn the postcard over in my hands. Sure enough, it's the same shade of red as the one for the personal assistant job at Empire Investments.

On reflex, I scan the table where I'd almost kissed Caelin MacGregor. Sure, that was an illusion. But submitting for the job was real enough.

Why haven't I gotten a response?

My logical self knows that it's too early to hear back on my application. That doesn't stop me from constantly checking my email.

I jam the postcard into my satchel and head back home. By the time I reach the Lucky Ladies, it's just past 3 a.m. I march past the empty warehouses leading up to the club. All the buildings seem to stare at me with broken-window eyes.

As I close in on the club, music wafts into the air. Technically, we're supposed to close at 2 a.m. In practice, the place doesn't empty out until sunrise. There are no neighbors to complain. And if anyone did? They'd have to answer to the owner, Konstantin.

As I close in on the main door, I repeat my regular mantra.

Act submissive.
Don't make eye contact.
Be invisible.

I saunter right past the bouncer and into the club. As a rule, the place is half-full even on the best nights. But tonight, the room is packed. That only happens when we have a new performer. Which we don't. I'd have noticed a new station in the dressing room. After all, that's my only route to reach the showers.

What's going on?

Seeing the crowd is such a shock, I stop focusing on being invisible. A hand clamps onto my shoulder.

It's Otto.

"Go to the empty warehouse next door. Wait for my signal."

"Hello, Otto," I state. "How are you this fine evening?"

"Konstantin is here," says Otto.

"That explains why you're busy tonight." Whenever Konstantin hits the club, there's always a pack of hangers-on. "Why do I need to hide? Maybe I should chat with Konstantin directly."

"He's here because he wants the final report on Ghost, or whatever his name is. You don't have dick. Willing to risk little Sashy-washy? "

"I hate you."

"Good, just get the fuck out of here."

I slip out the front door and back onto the street. This time, I'm careful to keep my inner mantra going.

I'm invisible. I'm invisible. I'm invisible.

I scale the fire escape on the brick warehouse next door. After pulling open a second-floor window, I crawl inside the deserted building. The place is a lot of broken tile floors, moldy plaster-board walls, and dust. I go downstairs until I reach a particular stretch of brick wall.

Once there, I listen.

If Otto is right, then Konstantin will want to inspect my

room. I set my satchel down and smile. Fortunately, my notes on Vice are safe in my bag.

Sure enough, Konstantin's voice easily carries through the wall.

"Where is she?" asks Konstantin.

"Eh, you know Lexa. She ran off to see her sick sister. Wah wah wah, get me my meds. Same old routine. She'll be there all night."

I flip an unladylike hand gesture toward the wall. *Otto is such a creep.*

Rustling noises sound. "Where are her gig notebooks?" That's Konstantin again.

"She burns them after each heist is over," replies Otto. "The one for Vice is probably with her now." Otto lets out an exaggerated sigh. "Lexa is such a pain in the ass. Every day, I have to kick that bitch's ass to make her work."

Now, I make nasty gestures with both hands. Sure, I know why Otto's doing this. He wants Konstantin to think I'm such a hassle, I need Otto around in order to produce. In other words, Otto is marking his territory with all the tact of a honey badger.

"Lexa did good on the Strauss job," says Konstantin. The subtext here is clear: I'm worth the hassle.

Take that, Otto.

I shouldn't get a rush just because Konstantin mentioned the Strauss job. Yet, I do. That was a juicy one. I found a shipping container filled with unmarked hundred-dollar bills, along with the perfect time to empty the thing. Because what thief would complain about someone else taking their illegal stuff?

Otto speaks again. "Are you here about Vice?"

"Da. When do I get the plan?"

"This Friday. That's rock solid."

"I don't want to hear that from you. Call Lexa."

"Why talk to her directly? That's why you have me. Build a direct line to her and it could ruin everything."

Konstantin lowers his voice in a way that makes it even easier for me to hear. "Anyone sniffing around here, looking for her?"

"Nah. Outside of her mom and sister, Lexa's got no one."

Wow, that's mean. Yet again, Otto proves himself to be an ass.

"Her cover is still solid, then?"

"Let me put it to you this way. Lexa's good for two things—bikini contests and stakeouts. She's ours."

A jolt of worry runs through me. Konstantin is worried that my cover is blown. That makes two of us.

"I mean it," declares Otto. "I know where that bitch is every second of every day. No one's following her. This operation is solid."

Konstantin doesn't say he believes Otto. But the big boss does change the subject. In our world, that's as good as a *yes*.

"There's a reunion for Paxton High," says Konstantin. "Tomorrow night. Midtown. It's something I'm running with Silver Pharma. You are not welcome. Same with Lexa."

"Hold on," says Otto. "Word on the street is that Silver Pharma's recruiting humans for enhancements. For years, I've been your loyal soldier. Is this reunion recruiting folks for strength or something? It's my turn. I'm going."

A rustle of fabric sounds, combined with a kind of gargling noise. No question about it. Someone's getting strangled. My money is on Otto.

"You don't tell me what to do." Konstantin's voice carries the edge of a growl. "Get me the intel I need by Friday. And if you hit Midtown tomorrow? I'll skin you alive."

"Yes, sir." Otto's voice sounds like he's speaking while gasping for air. That fact shouldn't give me any joy. But it does, just a little.

Another rustling sound follows. Konstantin must be releasing Otto. A flip of paper sounds. "He's your share on the Strauss heist," says Konstantin.

Otto flicks through bills. "Is this right? My guys saw a lot of cash in that container."

"Too bad they didn't get there first," says Konstantin. "My team saw a lot less."

"Of course. Must be a problem with my *intel*."

By saying *intel*, Otto's talking about me. And the information I gave him about the Strauss heist was perfect. If Otto's guys are too slow, that's on them.

How many payments have I missed because Otto sucks on execution?

"Remember," says Konstantin in a warning tone. "If anything changes with Lexa, you let me know."

"Yes, sir."

Footsteps sound as someone walks away. Must be Konstantin.

At this point, my eavesdropping has gotten me three key pieces of information. One, there's a Paxton High reunion in Midtown tomorrow night. Two, Vice will probably show up. And three, Otto has cash. I need to catch him before he blows it on something stupid.

Once I'm sure Konstantin is gone, I return to my room. Otto is still there.

"Did you hear anything?" asks Otto.

"Through a brick wall? I waited by a front window in the warehouse. When I saw Konstantin walk past, I came back here."

It's a lie, but I've already come up with a plan. If Vice is at that party, then he won't be in his apartment. I'm going into the Nouveau Palais at last. And I don't want Otto interfering. No matter what my boss said to Konstantin, Otto has zero control over where I go and what I do.

"Good." Otto hands over a stack of bills. "Here's your cut on the Strauss job."

I make a quick count. "Hey, this isn't enough for rent and Sash's meds."

"Add in your two hundred in winnings from the bikini contest, and it is."

A heavy sense of loathing settles into my bones. "You're unbelievable."

"Do we have to do this again?" asks Otto. "You complain, I threaten your sister, and grift goes on."

Otto sizes me up from head to toe. I wait for him to pass along Konstantin's message about avoiding Midtown. That's not what happens. Instead, Otto waddles away while flipping through his wad of money.

I toy with the idea that Otto is setting me up. If I go to Midtown, I might end up dead. Yet, that's not in Otto's best interest. If I'm not getting Konstantin's warning, it's for one reason: Otto sucks at his job.

I plunk onto my bed and pull my laptop from under my pillow. It takes a little surfing, but I soon find a chat board about the Midtown party.

Come to Club Castle tomorrow night, 8 p.m.
Paxton High School reunion
See you there!
-Devon and Shay

I shiver. I remember those two. Devon and Shay were the angry girls who hung out in the back corner of every classroom. They were besties with Vice.

I smile from ear to ear. Finally, I know when Vice will be out of his apartment. I've broken into buildings like Vice's before.

I'll do it again tomorrow night, no problem.

25

LEXA

5:04 p.m.

And Vice is still in his apartment.

For my part, I sit at my favorite table by the window of Big Apple Coffee. My hands tremble from the combination of not enough sleep and too much caffeine. And I've been watching Vice's apartment for the last eight hours straight. One question overtakes my thoughts.

What's Vice doing, exactly?

Although Vice keeps the window blinds drawn, I can still make out silhouettes. Based on the erratic light patterns, Vice is probably watching movies.

Until he isn't.

Every so often, strange shadows appear on the blinds. Based on the patterns, it looks as if Vice's waltzing with a massive octopus… or making shadow puppets with kitchen utensils. Talk about strange. I've been staking out buildings for seven years. This is a first.

Penny stops by with a fresh pot of coffee. "Need a warm up?"

"Sure thing."

What happens next seems to go in slow motion. Behind

Penny, a customer rises from his seat and bumps Penny's elbow. It reality, it only takes a second for the full pot to splash me with java. In my mind, every drop moves in slow motion.

I'm doused.

"Oh, no!" Penny gasps. "I'm so sorry."

I stand up and shake the extra liquid off my notebook. "It's okay."

"That was really hot. Are you burned? Should we get a doctor?"

Pulling up my sleeve, I check my front arm. There are a few red spots which are already healing up. "It's fine."

"That can't be right." Penny leans in for a better look. "You don't have a mark." She gazes at me like I just sprouted an extra eye. "That should have done something."

I shrug. "Maybe it wasn't as hot as you thought." I pull a soaking wet twenty-dollar bill from my pocket and set it on the tabletop.

"You don't have to do that." Penny still grabs the cash, though.

"I'll be back later." I stride out of the coffee shop and start the trek back to Lucky Ladies.

While I'm happy for the excuse to stop watching Vice, I'm not-so-pleased that my outfit is ruined. I still plan to break into Vice's place tonight. The green dress I'm wearing perfectly mimics the uniform of the cleaning staff at the Nouveau Palais. Maybe if I get back quickly enough, I can find a replacement outfit in the club dressing room. You'd be amazed at the wide array of outfits strippers leave behind.

Something has to work. I'm not missing my chance to inspect Vice's safe.

An hour later, I slide out of the performer's shower at Lucky Ladies. It's late afternoon, so the first of the talent should be here.

Wrapping myself in a towel, I step into the dressing room. The performers get ready in a small space crammed with row after row of make-up stations. Roller-racks of clothing line the far wall.

Sure enough, someone's already at her dressing station. Cartier. She's in her early forties with wide brown eyes and long dark hair. If my mother weren't a washout, she might look like Cartier.

"Hey, honey." Cartier winks at me. "What're you doing here?"

"I need a disguise to *break and enter* tonight. What about you? It's early for your set." Cartier is an old favorite. Her regulars don't show up until well after 2 am.

"Dinner with grandma tonight," answers Cartier. "The old bitch can't last much longer. Unless I look presentable, I'll be written out of the will." She nods to the seat beside her. A simple red dress hangs over the chair's back. I've seen that outfit before.

"You're not wearing this," I say with a sly grin. "It's from Sunny's old Nancy Reagan strip tease." I pick up the dress, grasp either side of the neckline, and pull. The snaps along the seams pop, turning one dress into two halves.

Sunny was an odd duck.

"Are you planning to impress Grandma with an extra show over dessert?" I ask.

Cartier giggles. "Absolutely."

"Well, she'll leave everything to you then." I reassemble the dress and then head over to the clothing racks.

Cartier rises. "Tell me you're finally dressing up."

"I need to look like cleaning staff."

"French maid?" asks Cartier.

I pull a loose green dress off the rack. "This could work."

Cartier rolls her eyes. "If you'd ask for my help, I can make you a sexy maintenance worker." Rising, Cartier pulls a different red dress from the rack. "This one is perfect for you. It's a knock-out." She thrusts the red gown toward me. "Take a look. You know you want to."

And she's right. I grab the gown and set it against my body. It's a simple red sheath with a built-in tulle wrap.

"You're right, Cartier. This is pretty."

"Just put it on for one minute." Cartier rushes back to her dressing table and picks up a few items. "Let me add a little blush, too."

I grip the hanger more tightly. "Why bother? I don't know where I'd ever wear something like this."

"Ever heard of the House of Music?"

"Surprisingly enough, I have."

"Ooh, Lexa! You could go there and have your pick of handsome men. Then, you can get laid, good and proper."

I mock-gasp. "Cartier!"

"You need to lose that V-card."

Not that I'm telling Cartier this, but that is not happening. Ever since Legacy Day at Paxton High, it's been a non-stop battle to keep Sash alive. If I'm being honest with myself, it's a fight that only ends when either Sash or I are six feet under.

Romance is out of the question.

I reset the dress on the rack. "Maybe another night."

Cartier gestures across the dressing table. "If you ever change your mind, help yourself."

"Thanks."

I head for the door... and Vice.

26

CAELIN

6:43 pm.

On a street of bland concrete skyscrapers, the headquarters for Silver Pharma stands out as a pristine spike of white marble. It towers above the landscape like a scalpel about to slice through Manhattan. I approach the doors.

Locked. Again.

For the second time in as many hours, I fail to enter the building. Although it's a weekday, the place appears deserted. Even the lobby security guard is gone. Clearly, the Gray Woman—or rather, Dr. Silver—is up to something.

Best to make something clear.

I focus on the nearest security camera. "I'll return tomorrow at dawn. Open these doors, or I'll enter one of your old caves and summon you." To emphasize the point, I grab the bronze handle so tightly, it snaps in two. "I can enter this place at any time. My patience has limits."

My shoulders tighten in frustration. Back when I was king, I saw the Gray Woman as a supernatural creature beyond logic or time. Over the last millennium, she's become more of a disappointment than a goddess.

A memory appears. I'm back in the cave in my old realm. I kneel on the sandy floor. Elisava's body is still warm and in my arms. The Gray Woman stares down at us.

In honor of your wife and child, I shall try to help your people survive.

For centuries, I waited for the Gray Woman to make good on her promise. Nothing happened.

Leaving Silver Pharma behind, I take a stroll around Manhattan and inspect my properties. It's satisfying to walk through places where I have skeleton keys that can access anything. I inspect two high rises, an office building, and one parking garage.

It's late in the day by the time I reach the Nouveau Palais. This time, the doorman allows me inside.

"Good evening, Mr. MacGregor."

"And to you."

Once inside, I scan my property. The pink granite floors are clean and glistening. The molded plaster ceiling is free from dust. And the oil paintings on the walls are pristine copies of impressionist masters.

My phone buzzes with a text from Konstantin.

U R in my bldg

I crack a smile. *That's right. Konstantin rents the penthouse suite here.* Not that he's paid anything yet. I type a quick reply.

Nae, you're in MY building

Perhaps it's because I'm a thousand years old, but I can't follow this trend for abbreviation. If it's still popular in two hundred years, then I'll consider it. My phone buzzes again.

In p house. Come up

Konstantin has more than a dozen apartments in and around the city. Now, my friend's waiting in the same building that Lexa's watching. Not a coincidence.

And if I'm being honest with myself, it's no coincidence that I'm here, either. Ever since Lexa and I locked gazes outside the coffee shop, my thoughts keep circling back to her. Over the past few days, I've done a little research of my own. Konstantin has Lexa staking out Prudence's brother, Vice. In turn, Vice lives on the second floor of this building. In some corner of my mind, I know I've been checking my other buildings just to have a reason to come here sooner rather than later.

Minutes pass before I saunter into the penthouse suite. The place is a lot of wood floors and not much else. I turn to Konstantin. He wears black dress pants and a white collared shirt. For him, this is really dressing up.

"We need to talk." Konstantin folds his arms over his chest. "This building holds an apartment that I asked Lexa to watch. That's why I'm here. What about you?"

"It's *my* building," I reply. "You merely rent this space." I scan a nearby stretch of wall. "Bloodstains go against the lease, you know. Find another place for your interrogations."

"And that's why you're here? Checking for bloodstains?"

"I'm inspecting some of my properties. The Nouveau Palais is on the list. It's all part of the boring side of maintaining a fortune."

Konstantin stares at me for a long minute. I can picture his mind sorting through every fact about me, Vice, and Lexa. At last, he breaks the silence.

"I checked into things. Lexa's not at risk. Otto keeps her safe."

The smart move here would be to act as if I don't care about Lexa. It seems when it comes to this human, I'm not too clever.

"How does that work?" I ask. "Lexa lives miles away from Otto."

A smug gleam shines in Konstantin's eyes. "She's fine. I checked things out personally."

Jealousy flares through me. Somehow, I'm, able to push the emotion aside and continue to appear calm.

"Did you see Lexa?" I ask.

"Nah, I talked to Otto. Lexa was hiding nearby. I could sense her heartbeat through the walls. Could scent her as well."

This time, my level of jealousy goes into the stratosphere. My hands ball into fists as I manage to speak a single word. "And?"

"She's fine, like I said."

Waves of protective rage move through my body. How can this discussion bother me so much? Lexa is a human woman. I interact with her kind as little as possible. If they get too obsessive, then I send them away before they hurt themselves. I never get jealous.

"What're you glaring at me about?" Konstantin nods slowly. "Ah, I get it."

I brace my shoulders. Here it comes. Konstantin knows I'm interested in Lexa. *He'll lose his mind.* I scan the room, contemplating the best attack vectors.

"You know what I'm thinking, don't you?" ask Konstantin.

"Do I?"

"Come on. You've always been King Caelin the Clever, the man who hoards both gold and secrets. Now, for the first time, I have the upper hand in the form of better people and my own money. It bothers you."

Konstantin's theory is both wrong and revealing. Contrary to what my friend thinks, I love that's he's no longer constantly begging me for cash. And the fact that Konstantin thinks I care about besting him says far more about him than me.

I rock on my heels and debate about telling Konstantin the truth. As soon as the idea appears, I set it aside. Admitting my interest in Lexa would set off Konstantin's competitive instincts. And the hallucination part would make me seem ready for a trip to the Gray Woman myself.

A dark thought strikes me. What if the Gray Woman's latest enhancements trap bloodkin men like me in hallucinations?

"Let's change the subject," I declare.

"I knew it!" Konstantin grins. "You can't stand to lose."

"Oh, I've lost plenty."

"You're right." Konstantin's smile falters. "We both have."

There's a connection between us. Not like what happened with me and Lexa, but a shared sorrow. We both carry a soul-deep weight that never lightens. *Elisava.*

"I have it," says Konstantin. "How about we hit the Bold Tsarina? It's our best club in the city. What do you think?"

"Haven't seen it yet."

"Are you kidding? This place marks our last great investment and you can't bother to go? For shame."

"I'll do so another time."

"Good."

"For now, I better check that boiler."

"Right. And I'm off for a recruiting event in Midtown. It's to help the Gray Woman. Want to join me?"

"Nae."

"Then, what are you going to do?"

"Check the boiler and leave. I am not helping you recruit humans for the Gray Woman."

Konstantin sighs. "You're stubborn as fuck."

"Aye." And I do head down to the basement to inspect the boiler.

Because, once I'm done there, I have another room to visit as well.

LEXA

*a*fter I leave the Lucky Ladies, I take a new route to the Nouveau Palais. It means an extra-long train ride, but I want to be sure no one's following me. Eventually, I march toward the entrance to Vice's home.

Up close, the Nouveau Palais towers higher than I remember. Every inch of red brick is carved with intricate patterns. Bronze filigree frames the windows. A wide green awning covers the main doors. On reflex, I keep straightening my green dress and repositioning my satchel. All of a sudden, it's hard to pull in enough air.

You can do this, Lexa.

As I close in on the entrance, a guard in a green suit jacket opens the door.

"Good evening, Miss."

I'd planned my outfit with care. But when it comes to what I'll say? Not so much.

"Yeah," I say lamely.

The guard scans me from head to toe. Another legit worker steps right past me and into the building.

"Hey, Rodney," she says.

"Good evening, Clara," he replies.

Oh, hell. My green dress doesn't match the rest of the staff. Standing around doesn't make the situation any better. Lifting my chin, I try to bluff it out and walk inside.

The guard moves to stand in my path. "Hold on."

My pulse beats so hard, I hear a whooshing sound. I set my hand on my neck. My own heart races faster than what sounds in my head. A jolt of shock moves through me.

It isn't my heartbeat I'm hearing.

This must be another hallucination. Who hears someone else's heartbeat in their mind?

"Are you here to visit someone?" asks the guard slowly.

This is why I do surveillance and let someone else handle the adrenaline surge of active ops. I'm not the type who can charm myself out of situations.

I gesture across myself. "I clean apartments."

"Really."

"Green dress," I add lamely.

Not my best comeback.

"You don't work here," says the guard. "Leave."

The heartbeat sounds louder. I lean into the sound. "I can go inside." And I follow up that thought with a different version of Mom's inner mantra.

Let me pass. Let me pass. Let me pass.

The guard steps back, allowing me to step by. I don't wait for a formal invitation. I march right into the building and head for the stairwell. It's a short hike to the second floor.

Minutes later, I stand before the door to Vice's department. I've watched his place enough to know what kind of lock pick to use. I'm inside within seconds.

The place is pretty empty. A leather couch is the only furnishing in the living room... And it's trashed. The room looks as if someone decided to swipe a Samurai sword along the walls and furniture. Green slime oozes from the cut marks.

I shiver, remembering the odd shadows on the closed window blinds. What the hell has Vice been up to in here?

Not sure I want to know.

And it's not why I'm here, either.

I explore the bedroom. The place looks untouched. Someone even made the bed. The curtain is pulled aside, revealing the wall safe.

It's closed.

Over the years, I've gotten good at guessing safe combinations from a distance. I'm pretty sure I know how to open this one. It takes a few tries, but I'm able to unlock the safe.

Sweat beads on my forehead as I pull the safe open.

When I saw Vice open the safe, it was crammed with gold bars. My body trembles with surprise.

This time, the safe is empty.

I step inside the safe itself. It's been cleaned out. The picture that was stuck to the inside of the safe door is gone as well. A flash of white catches my eye. A scrap of paper sits on the floor. Leaning over, I scoop up the small document.

It's a picture of me.

The pic shows me in Big Apple Coffee, sitting at my fave seat by the window. My heart sinks.

Vice knows who I am. I'm exposed.

I've been so careful to be the secret earner for Konstantin's organization. *What a disaster.* My head feels wobbly on my shoulders. I shuffle back into the bedroom.

And things get worse.

Someone sneaks up behind me. The next thing I know, I'm pressed against the nearest stretch of wall. An electric charge of fear runs through my nervous system.

It's happened. I've been discovered. Someone's out to hurt Konstantin. Who is it? Italians? Irish?

I do surveillance, I don't battle thugs. At this point, I should dissolve into tears. Instead, something inside me awakens. An ancient power streams through my veins. Rage overtakes my mind.

"What are you doing here?" I ask.

"It's *my* building, lass."

That voice is low, rumbling, and haunting my dreams. My anger instantly turns into something else. I know who this is.

"Caelin," I whisper.

When he next speaks, Caelin's warm breaths fans over my bare neck. "Aye."

Lights flash before utter darkness surrounds us. Any reflection from the streetlights vanishes. My breath catches.

A moment ago, the bedroom blinds were closed. Somehow they've now opened. Moonlight shines into the room. Cool tendrils of mist twist across the floor and around our bodies. I'm still pressed against the wall.

Only now, I'm naked.

So is Caelin.

I can't see the man, but I feel the hard planes of his chest and thighs against my back. My legs now stand more than shoulder-length apart. I sense Caelin's length pressing outside my entrance, all velvet skin over steely muscle. His rough breaths sound in my ear, making my insides twist with desire.

Caelin slides his warm palm down my arm. Everywhere he touches, there's a trail of want. How can this be happening again?

Not sure I care anymore.

CAELIN

J expected to find certain things upon entering Vice's apartment, such as gold, guns, or drugs. But someone sneaking around in the dark?

Definitely *not* on the list.

The moment I crossed the threshold, I could sense a second heartbeat nearby. I stalked into the bedroom to find what seemed like someone from the cleaning service. I pinned the stranger to the wall.

The moment we were close, I caught a familiar scent. *Cedar and musk.* Lexa.

"What are you doing here?" she asked.

"It's my building," I replied.

"Caelin," she whispered.

Once again, the world changed. Lights went out. Mist rolled in. Moonlight shone. And the two of us became naked.

And that's where we are now.

I've always prided myself on being someone who controls their passions. It's how I send my soeurs away before they get too close. Or anyone else, for that matter.

In this moment, with Lexa's naked skin pressing against mine, desire floods every corner of me. Little by little, I slide my palm down her arm and just outside the swell of her breasts. Her breathing turns low and tight.

I want this more than anything.

And that's why I step away.

Flights flash. Blinds cover the window once more. Mist vanishes. Whatever spell this is, it ends.

I'm clothed again. Lexa is back inside the opened safe.

Every instinct tells me to return to her. Logic dictates that I must leave. Lexa is human. If I stay, red madness will take her mind long before it drains her body.

I slip back out of the apartment. There's no more questioning the truth. Clearly, Lexa's been enhanced to cause hallucinations in bloodkin. She's dangerous.

All the more reason to keep my word to the Gray Woman. First thing tomorrow, I'm back at Silver Pharma.

With that resolution, I walk away.

29

LEXA

Did that even happen?

My legs feel boneless beneath me, so I lean against the safe wall. My body's still on fire from *whatever that was* with Caelin.

I picture Mr. Brookhollow from Paxton High. What would he say? The high school hallucinations were my mind's way of trying to process the fire that took our family's California home. I spent the last seven years in a set routine. It's not a ton of laughs, but it is safe. Expected.

No surprises. No hallucinations. *That's the key.*

Reaching into my satchel, I pull out the picture Vice left on the safe floor. This creep has been watching me for a while now. Haven't I been sensing someone's eyes on me? That must be Vice. On some level, I have felt the danger behind his surveillance.

And danger brings hallucinations.

I scan the image of me sitting at my favorite table in the Big Apple Coffee. I wear black pants and a matching shirt. That's not my typical outfit. Normally, I try to blend, and that means gray.

Another realization tingles down my spine. I recall the day I wore all black. It was the first time I hallucinated about Caelin.

Mr. Brookhollow's advice makes more sense by the minute. At the same time I was getting visions of sexy-time with Caelin, Vice is snapping pictures of me from the shadows. Part of me knew I was in danger. I went back to an old habit: hallucinating.

Disappointment and relief churn through me. I feel better knowing that there's a logical explanation to what happened. Still, it hurts to know everything with Caelin's just an illusion.

I flip the image over. Things get worse. A message is written on the back.

Konstantin's earner. 1 M bounty.

There's a price on my head? That can't be right. Vice must be playing with me. Still, I can't take that risk. I set the picture inside my satchel. Whatever's happening, moping inside an empty safe won't fix it. I need a plan.

Lights flash again. I'm inside a bright white room. Two long silver tables sit nearby. Bodies lay on top of each. My blood chills.

Oh, no.

I've seen this place before. Sash and I were lying on tables just like these—and in a chamber identical to this one—only we were little and in hospital gowns.

I inch closer to the tables. It's not Sash and I laying on top of them, but Vice and some woman with red hair. A lady in a lab coat enters the room.

I shiver. I know this doctor. No matter how hard I try, I can't recall where I met her before.

The doctor stands beside Vice's table. He starts to sit up.

"Keep down," says the doctor. "When you need to move, I'll tell you." She picks up his wrist and runs her fingertips along his skin. "Your latest enhancement is coming along well."

I slip closer to the doctor. She has silver hair and eyes. Even her pale skin carries a gray hue. Somehow, I know that if I could pull her hair back, she'd have pointed ears.

The female patient pipes up. "I want my enhancement as well. How can you check him for something new when I've waited years for anything at all?"

The doctor steps over to the second patient. "We've covered this before. You'll get what I tell you, when I tell you."

"I want strength," says the woman.

Damn, they both look familiar. A hazy memory comes into focus. I'm in a cave, fighting against some kind of ropes that tie me down. These two were there. Names appear. Prudence and Viceroy.

The doctor raises a massive syringe high above her head and plunges it into Prudence's heart.

"You'll get this," says the doctor.

I press my fingertips to my temples, as if I can shove this hallucination out of my mind.

"This can't be happening," I whisper.

The doctor immediately looks over in my direction. "Hello." She eyes me carefully. "So, this is your magic."

"Me? Magic?"

"Come back to me another day," says the doctor. "I've no time for you now."

Light flashes once more. I'm back in the safe again.

"That's it," I announce. "Put a fork in me, I'm done here."

If danger triggers my hallucinations, then going somewhere I feel safe. That should stop them.

Thank you, Mr. Brookhollow.

I head off toward the exit, repeating Mom's old mantra the entire time.

Head down.
Don't make eye contact.
Be invisible.

30

CAELIN

*I*t's dawn. As promised, I march toward the entrance to the Silver Pharma building. Part of me hopes that the Gray Woman keeps the doors sealed so I can break in and do battle. When I was king, every week brought a new assault.

A small smile rounds my mouth. It's been too long between fights.

As I close in on the building, the doors swing open on their own. Two young ladies come out. They're both human but too perfect for that status. Both have dark hair, brown eyes, and identical couture hoodies. One wears a necklace that spells out the name, *Devon*.

No doubt, these are the latest recruits for the Gray Woman's vampire enhancements. In this case, it's for beauty.

"Such a pleasure to see you," says Devon. "I'm Devon and this is Shay."

Shay frowns. "You said I could introduce us this time."

I notice a familiar patch on the shoulder of Shay's pink jacket. "You're a recruiter." In other words, they're bringing other humans into Silver Pharma for enhancements, same as Konstantin.

"We're both recruiters," explains Devon.

"He asked *me* the question," whispers Shay. "We're Silver Pharma Girls, Gamma Chapter. We're influencers for their latest beauty programs."

Devon snaps her fingers. "You just missed it. We held a recruiting event last night. You should join the next one. You could help us, just like Konstantin does."

"Shut up," says Shay. "We're not supposed to talk about the K man."

"I'm here to see Dr. Silver," I state. "Excuse me."

I stride into the building. The two humans follow. "We're supposed to show you to the doctor's waiting room," offers Shay.

"That won't be necessary." Reaching out with my vampire senses, I connect to the humans' pulses and think a command.

Do not follow me.

The two women walk away, leaving me free to navigate the maze of hallways that wind through Silver Pharma. Everything is pristine, white, and empty. Eventually, I find my way to the Gray Woman's lab. It's a huge chamber lined with white tile. Long metal tables cover the floor. Glass containers and odd-shaped machines are everywhere.

The Gray Woman leans over a tray of small glass vials. "Hello, Caelin."

"Hello." I pause with my back to the table. This way, I can get a better look at her face. "You're up to something. Talk."

"My goals never change. Chaos, your Highness. Chaos."

"How did you enhance Vice?"

"I gave him some bloodkin skills for stealth."

"And Lexa Uznetsov? How did you enhance her?"

The Gray Woman blinks in what she assumes is an innocent way. "I don't know what you mean."

"You dug up a mindlock demon. Did you give Lexa enhancements to cause hallucinations?"

"That is one question I will never answer."

"In other words, *yes*. When did you enhance Lexa?"

"Poor King Caelin. You aren't asking the right questions."

"I'm in no mood for games," I state.

"Follow me and I'll give you a hint about what I really mean. This way." She crosses across the tile floor.

I stay put. "I don't wish to be toyed with."

The Gray Woman pauses. "I vow that what I'm about to show you will be useful… eventually."

At this point, I'd love to go medieval and simply attack. After all, I keep my obelisk dagger handy for just such occasions. But, the Gray Woman would turn liquid and vanish before I could get close. My best chance for the truth is to see what she wishes to show.

I follow the Gray Woman through a heavy metal door and into a massive space. Here, the walls are metal and covered in frost. A maze of huge ice blocks covers the floor. I've been here before. This is cold storage for Silver Pharma. The Gray Woman built it in the 1920's. Ever since then, she's been chucking iced-over test subjects in here.

The Gray Woman gestures across the massive space. "These are my future experiments. Do you know how this works?"

"You only use live subjects," I offer. "And if that can't happen right away, they get iced." I step around the tall blocks. Inside each one stands a shadowy humanoid figure. "I remember when you iced over your first human. 1922, I believe."

"Something like that."

I scan a new row of ice blocks. "I don't see any primal daemons."

The Gray Woman widens her eyes in what's supposed to be another innocent look. "Primal daemons?"

"You've been digging them up for years. At least, the mindlock daemon should be in here by now. You promised a hint. What is it—are you giving new injections to enhance humans?"

The Gray Woman smirks. "You're still not asking the right question."

I lace my fingers behind my neck and think things through. *Perhaps my question is too broad.* "Are you somehow enhancing humans with the ability to cause hallucinations? Not by an injection, but a spell?"

"Wrong. wrong, wrong."

I think about Konstantin's request. "Does this have to do with the Midtown event last night? Is this your way of asking for my help?"

"Good question. The answer is no. And that's all the hints I'll give you for now."

The Gray Woman winks, transforms into water, and then seeps into the floor. This has happened before. It's an elemental daemon's way of saying, *conversation over.*

As I head for the door, I shake my head. Why did I ever think this talk would be helpful? The Gray Woman loves to confuse. I'm back to my original plan.

If anyone will tell me what these hallucinations mean, it will be Lexa herself.

CAELIN

*a*fter leaving the Gray Woman, I return to Empire Investments. I soon cross the threshold to my outer reception chamber. Prudence steps out from behind her desk. In some ways, she looks as she always does, from her neatly-styled red hair to her tailored tweed suit. In other ways, there's no missing the new aura of worry that surrounds her.

"We haven't had a chance to talk," says Prudence. "Not since…"

"I spoke to your brother in an alley?"

"Yes, that. I don't want you to think he's a criminal."

"I'm not the law. What happens with your family is always your own business."

"Oh. So, nothing else bothers you?"

I know what she's referring to here. The fact that Vice brought up Fyodor the Rus. And in truth, that irks me quite a lot. But it's not in my best interest to share that concern until I have a lot more information. In such situations, I find it best to answer a question with another question.

"Why would it concern me?"

"Of course, it wouldn't." She exhales. "I have those revenue reports for you. I set them into your viewing console."

"Thank you. Please set up calls with all the property management companies I work with in Manhattan. I believe there are five."

"Is there a problem?"

"My parking garage at the port authority is riddled with water damage. Tenants in my high rise on 57th street decided some load-bearing walls were blocking their *feng shui*. The top floor of the building is now unstable. The list goes on."

"I understand. I'll set up the calls directly."

"Thank you." I walk past the reception chamber into my meeting room. Hunter lounges on one of the long leather couches. He throws a small rubber ball up and down. Like always, he starts the conversation without greetings.

"I used my mind control to slip past Prudence," says Hunter. He wears his regular camo pants, black shirt, and hefty boots. "I'm nowhere near as good as you are, though. Did she tell you I was in here?"

"No. And what's—"

"—The red ball about? It's for stress. A human thing."

"You and your human trends." If Hunter's here, it's because his reconnaissance found something else. "Are we chatting in here or my inner office?"

"All the way, baby."

Which means Hunter has something important to report. My inner office is both sound and spell-proof.

I open a hidden door to my inner office and take a seat behind my real desk. Hunter drags a chair over, sits down, and kicks his feet onto the desktop.

"You don't mind, do you?" asks Hunter. He knows I don't care about boot marks. He's just dragging out the drama of his report. The man does have a unique sense of humor.

"In case you haven't noticed, I hire people to clean things."

Hunter purses his lips. "So, I guess you're wondering what I found?"

"No, I'm wondering how long you can drag this out."

"Can you get into your human resources system?"

"I can." I press a few of the keys embedded in my desktop. The wall of monitors comes to life. Our employee software system comes up across all the screens. "I've got it."

"Type in the words, Alexa Uznetsov."

I do. The screens update. "It says here, she applied for the open position as my personal assistant."

"The same person who delivers Sasha Uznetsov's meds also dropped off a postcard about that position."

"Meaning Vice." I click through a few more screens. "And Lexa is the only applicant in the last two years." I drum my fingers on the desktop and consider this news. "Prudence, what have you been doing?"

Hunter bobs his brows. "My question as well."

I tap more buttons on my console. The image of both the middle meeting room and reception chamber appear on the monitor wall.

"I'll go see Prudence," I state. "Track what happens on this monitor. And whatever I tell Prudence to do, make sure she does it."

"Aye. After this is over, will you kill Prudence?"

"Depends what she does. But based on how things are going? I'm guessing I'll have to."

"I only hope I'm there to see it, your Highness."

Turning, I head for reception. Sure enough, I find Prudence sitting at her desk in reception. She slaps on an over-bright smile. "How can I help you?"

"Let's talk about the personal assistant position. Where do we stand?"

"We've had some new applications. None are any good."

"One was from Alexa Uznetsov."

"Oh, I think I remember her now. I could bring her in next week."

"Why not tomorrow?"

"It's personal. I'm having some treatments. I'll be better able to handle it next week, if you don't mind."

Over the centuries, I've learned many things. One of them is when humans aren't telling the truth. And Prudence is lying right now.

"I can set it up myself," I state.

"But you're booked solid tomorrow."

I shrug. "I'll move things."

"On second thought, I can do this for you. When should I set up the appointment?"

"Tomorrow. 4 pm."

And I walk away.

LEXA

*a*fter the sexy hallucination in Vice's apartment, I head right back to Lucky Ladies. To fight unwanted visions, I need some comfort and familiarity.

Lucky Ladies is the best I'll get.

Once back, I head straight for my room and crash on the cot. To keep Otto scarce, I use what I call my *nuclear option.* In other words, I leave a tampon box on the floor outside my door.

Sure enough, Otto stays away.

I order Chinese food and surf the web. There are no visions of hot encounters with unattainable Scotsmen. This is a good thing.

There's some not-so-good stuff, too. I crack out multiple notebooks and scribble page after page about my current dilemma. Most of the sheets end up listing the same facts: Vice knows who I am, my cover is blown, and there's nothing I can do about it.

This goes on until sunrise. Normally, I have at least a few ideas on how to get out of any situation. My motto is, *despair is the last refuge of the unimaginative.*

There's always something you can do, even if it's to just keep trying.

That said, even I have to admit that I need help. After I slip into jeans and a T-shirt, I make my way over to Mom and Sash's place.

Yeah, I'm that desperate.

The bus and train rides to visit Mom and Sash have never been slower. Honestly, it's amazing how time inches by when you're pretty sure people are trying to kill you. Every shadow is Vice. Each click is someone readying their gun. Combined with my lack of sleep, it's amazing that I don't hallucinate. Considering how rough yesterday was, maybe I've hit my quota for the week.

Finally, I reach the door to my family's apartment. There are no meds hanging on the doorknob. I take that as a good sign. After unlocking the door, I find a lone letter sitting on the floor. I scoop it up and head inside.

Sash lays on the couch. She's awake and staring at nothing in particular. The cloud of cigarette smoke heading in from the kitchen means Mom is at home as well.

Sash sits up. "What's wrong?"

I sigh. "My cover is definitely blown."

Sash sits up and pats the now-open space beside her on the couch. "Details, Lexa."

I sit beside her. "One of my targets knows that I'm Konstantin's earner. There's already a price on my head."

Sash smiles. "I thought you were just checking if you were in danger. How can you be sure? Maybe you misunderstood."

Reaching into my satchel, I pull out the sheet of paper I got from the floor of Konstantin's safe. "I found this in the guy's apartment."

Sash scans the sheet and reads aloud. *"Konstantin's earner. 1 M bounty."* She frowns. "Does that mean what I think it means?"

Mom steps into the living room. "A million dollar bounty." She lets out a low whistle. "I'm surprised any of us are still breathing. Everyone thinks you live here. If people are at risk, it's us."

"We should run," says Sash. "I won't be the reason my family gets killed."

Mom and I share a look. "Running—" I begin.

"—Is not an option," finishes Mom.

I slump back on the couch. *This is impossible.* Without thinking, I twist at the envelope in my hands.

Mom nods toward the message. "What's that?"

"I found it by the door. Guess you dropped it after picking up the mail." I hand over the envelope.

Mom scans the front. "Huh. It's addressed to you."

I reach out in a way that clearly says, *gimmie.*

My mother doesn't hand the letter back. Instead, she tears it open. "It's dated today." Mom scans the contents. "This can't be right."

"What is it? Bill collectors again?"

"No, you're supposed to interview for a job." Mom's voice actually kicks up an octave. I haven't heard her this excited since I brought her a carton of cigs instead of a single pack. "You could be the next personal assistant to Caelin MacGregor."

"Sha. That can't be right." But even as I speak these words, my body trembles with excitement.

I forgot all about that job application.

"See for yourself." Mom hands over the letter. I look it over.

Once.

Twice.

Sure enough, Mom's correct.

It really is an invitation to interview with Caelin MacGregor. As in, the same guy I keep hallucinating about.

Mom peers over my shoulder. "What's the deal?"

"They want me to come in tomorrow, 4 p.m. sharp." I nibble my lower lip. "I don't know if this is the right move, though."

Mom sparks up a new cig. "What you need is leverage." She points her smoke toward the envelope in my grasp. "It's right there. With a job offer from Caelin, I can negotiate our exit with Otto and Konstantin."

"That's a long shot," I state.

"No, it's as good as done," says Mom. "MacGregor wants to fuck you."

I roll my eyes. "Mother."

"All I'm saying is that if MacGregor wants to fuck, you do it."

"Yeah, I understood the first time."

Mom pins me with a look of pure rage. "You're a plain-looking nobody. He's Caelin fucking MacGregor. And he's having lackeys hand-deliver messages under our doors. What do you have to offer him? Nothing but a quick hop in the sack. So, do that. But first, get a commit from Caelin for our safety. Then, I use it to make sure Konstantin does what's right."

I frown. "How can you make sure Konstantin does that?"

"Because I did it once before. We'd all be dead right now if I hadn't negotiated with Konstantin after Legacy Day."

"That wasn't Lexa's fault," says Sash gently. "Dad was stealing from Konstantin."

Mom ignores Sash to focus on me. "You hear me? Get the commit. Hit the sack. After that, you never see him again."

That rage I felt before percolates up again. For the first time in what feels like ever, I really confront Mom. "To begin with, Sash said something. We don't ignore her." I look to my sister. "Thanks for the vote of confidence." I refocus on my mother. "And what makes you think I won't stay and work for Caelin? Maybe I'll like that job better."

"Sorry, you can't handle a man like that." Mom stubs out her smoke. "He'll break you, honey. Ask for us to be safe. Take one roll in the sack. Run."

"There's so much to hate in what you just said, I don't know where to begin."

"You know I'm right, then," states Mom. "As the saying goes, good advice is never welcome. And I'm giving you good advice."

For a moment, Mom takes on a different look. Intelligent. Confident. Scheming. This side of my mother pops up every so often, and it makes my soul fill with worry.

"What's really going on here?" I ask.

The sophisticated mask falls away. "Nothing, like always." Mom shoves the letter back at me. "There's a phone number at the bottom to text the HR bitch and confirm that you'll be there."

"She might not be a bitch."

Mom rolls her eyes. "She'll be one, believe me. Just text the word *'confirm'* to her now, while I'm watching. That way, I can have one decent night's sleep. All I do is worry where our next dollar is coming from."

"Not that you earn anything yourself."

Mom narrows her eyes at me. "I made you, didn't I? That was serious work. You were a preemie pain in my ass."

Something inside me says she's lying. Anger heats my blood. "Bull."

"Text her."

Something rises up inside me. Most days, I feel like an unseen cog in a massive machine of someone else's making. Right now, I'm something else.

"You're railroading me into something," I counter. "Why should I be a complaint little nobody here?"

Mom points at the letter with her cig. "That's our ticket to safety. Don't fuck it up."

That word rings through my mind. *Safety.* If I feel secure again, the hallucinations will stop. This job is the best way to make that happen. I won't let Mom stop me from doing what's right. I'll hit this interview and nail it. If nothing else, I'll prove to myself that I control the hallucinations, not the other way around.

"Fine. I'll do it." I take out my cell, enter the number, and type in a single word.

'Confirmed.'

LEXA

4:01 p.m.

I sit in the heavy wooden chair across from the desk of Prudence MacGuire, head of Human Resources for Empire Investments. I'm in a pencil skirt and loose tunic top. Prudence sports the tightest-fitting brown suit I've ever seen. The woman looks like a sausage about to burst from its casing. And that level of make up? I've seen circus clowns with less foundation.

Minutes pass while Prudence flicks through the stack of papers before her. Everything in this office carries the same red woodgrain pattern, from the walls to the floor. As for Prudence herself, she's pale-skinned with dark red hair that's pulled back into a tight bun. When I squint really hard, Prudence blends into the wood paneling so much, she becomes nothing but a floating head with dark brown eyes.

Kinda funny, actually.

Part of me knows I shouldn't be squinting during a job interview, especially one this important.

A nasal female voice breaks up my thoughts.

"Excuse me. Excuse me. EXCUSE ME."

I blink hard and refocus. *Right, I'm having an interview with Prudence.* I force on a smile. "Yes?"

"I asked you a question." Prudence narrows her button eyes at me, a movement which makes her whole face crinkle up. "A question!"

I make my grin wider somehow. "Do you mind asking again?"

"I said, your name is Alexa Uznetsov."

"Yes. And that's not a question."

Prudence taps her pen onto the top sheet on her desk. "It says here, you're twenty-four years old. Five foot four inches. Brown hair and blue eyes."

"Right again." *And that's still not a question.* Although, I'm somehow able to keep that thought to myself this time.

"And your measurements are 35-24-37." She crinkles her nose as if smelling something awful. "Your ass is rather large."

Prudence has been so fussy up until now, I'm taken aback. "What did you say?"

At this point, I've decided one thing. This woman hates me. My HR nemesis keeps right on going as if I didn't say a thing. I'm disliking her more by the second.

"Alexa, may I call you Lexa?"

I try to keep my mouth shut. *This is for Sash.* I need to stay cool. *I can't.*

"You just insulted my ass, so I guess we can *both* use nick-names here, Pru."

If my words upset Madame HR, she doesn't show it. "Strip down."

"What?"

"Take off your top and skirt."

This is like a bad dream. It's all happening, just like Mom predicted. Prudence is some kind of corporate madam, inspecting me for MacGregor. I should follow Mom's instructions. Strip down. Play along.

Too bad I suck at that kind of thing.

I fold my arms over my chest. "No. This is supposed to be a legit business."

If I'm being totally honest, there are other reasons to hold my ground. Namely, I wore my period underwear today. It's not that time of the month; I'm just really behind on laundry. A girl must have standards.

"MacGregor needs to uphold certain levels of beauty with his employees."

"That's so illegal, it isn't even funny." And thanks to Otto, that's the fifth time I've said those words this week.

Prudence pulls out a fresh stack of papers. "According to our research, you don't mind stripping down to your undies. You did it last Saturday night at a bikini contest at the Lucky Ladies Lounge."

There are two issues about this. First, it's totally true. Second, how could she know this?

"Do you have someone following me?" I ask.

"Of course," says Prudence smoothly. "We do this for all potential, uh, employees. Strip."

Some part of me demands that I just go along with this. It's a voice that sounds a lot like my mother. And Mom's not alone in complaining about how I suck at being a follower. Otto's always getting on me about that, too.

I should take off my shirt.

Now.

Nope, not happening.

Instead, I kick my legs forward and cross them at the heels. "The answer's still no."

"The people at Empire Investments all come from the best bloodlines. They're supernaturally beautiful. It's easier on huma —" She clears her throat. "It's easier on employees if they fit in when it comes to appearances."

"Did you almost call me *a human*?" I roll my eyes. "What a

pack of attitudes around here. Like winning the genetic lottery gives you extra rights or something." I rise to leave, but notice a dish of mints on Pru's desk. I grab a handful for later. "I'm gone."

"The job pays $100,000," says Prudence.

I turn and march toward the door. "Not enough."

"That's each month."

I stop in place. *A hundred grand every thirty days. That's a lot of money.* With that kind of cash, I could maybe negotiate Sash's meds directly from Silver Pharma. And if I stay for nine months, I might even get a regular apartment with actual bedrooms where my sister and I can live together.

But walking around in my underwear during a job interview? Prudence didn't ask me if I could type, for crying out loud. *Talk about your red flags.*

"I can read hallway signs, you know," I begin. "This little office is supposed to be for the personal assistant. You've got a pretty nameplate on the desk, but you're the HR chick. Which means I could be replacing you… and you have issues with that. Which is why you brought me in here at four o'clock when no one's around. My guess? Caelin MacGregor isn't even here."

"How insightful of you to notice my discomfort," says Prudence. "But it's not that I worry about a replacement. It's more that…" She stands and folds her arms over her chest. Somehow, that movement doesn't pop the seams on her jacket. "There are rumors you work for the infamous criminal, Konstantin."

My eyes widen. *If this random person knows I work for the Bratva, who doesn't?*

"Let's try this over again," says Prudence smoothly. "Why don't you come back in a week? I'll be more prepared to deal with your unique, ah, employment history at that time."

I do a double take. "My unique history? Who do you think you work for? Caelin MacGregor has done his share of illegal stuff."

"How dare you? It's time that you lef—"

Hidden speakers come to life with a low hiss. A man's voice reverberates across the room. "Send her in."

My insides twist with desire and shock. I know that voice. The speaker's tone is deep, rolling, and laced with a heavy Scottish brogue.

Caelin.

So this *really is* an interview. The money is beyond good. And it's clearly getting to be common news how I work for Konstantin. Still, there are principles at work here, like the fact that Prudence is only putting on a show. This job is sketchy as hell. My shoulders tighten with frustration.

At this point, I should think about my family or sanity. But again, my damn impulse control issues get in the way. I step around in a circle and stare at the ceiling. "Caelin, is that you?"

"Aye."

Prudence crumples to her knees. "Forgive her rudeness, your Majesty."

I decide to ignore Prudence because that *kneeling-thing* she's doing right now? So. Weird. Instead, I talk to the ceiling once more. "You've got a lot of nerve, Caelin."

I brace my shoulders, waiting for Prudence or Caelin to end the interview.

That isn't what happens.

34

CAELIN

The moment sears into my mind.

I stand before the wall of monitors in my inner office. Video streams in, showing various angles of the reception room.

One monitor displays Prudence on her knees. My employee knows she screwed up. Prudence is supposed to greet job applicants and show them into the central meeting room. Asking them to strip is not company policy.

On another display, Lexa stands with her hands on her hips and fire in her eyes. Her last words still ring in my ears.

"You've got a lot of nerve, Caelin."

When Prudence first snapped at Lexa, I almost marched into reception and set my Vice President of HR in her place.

Lexa beat me to it. Many times.

While meeting with Prudence, Lexa has proclaimed that her *ass has been insulted* and has announced that employees of Empire Investments tote around a *pack of attitudes*.

It's the most fun I've had in ages.

When I first locked eyes with Lexa, she was on a stakeout for Konstantin. Something about her inner grit and resolution connected with me. In our second encounter, Lexa and I ended up naked in the dark. Desire burned through me.

Up to this point, Lexa has embodied persistence and passion. Now, I'll add humor and wit into the mix. I like it very much indeed.

All of which is why I press a series of buttons on my desktop console. Over in reception, a hidden door swings open. On the video feed, Lexa fixes her gaze on the new entrance. Her eyes shine with interest, but she doesn't step any closer.

I press another button on my console. "Come on in, lass. I won't bite."

Lexa steels her spine and steps toward the passageway for the middle chamber. I click the button that closes the door behind her. And I keep the microphone to the reception room open. Without a doubt, Prudence will now have commentary.

Sure enough, Prudence stares into a nearby camera. "I would never contradict you around others," she says. "But this is folly. Lexa needs time to adjust to the idea of this interview. If we could just bring her back next week—"

"Not an option," I state. "Why don't you take the rest of the afternoon off?"

Prudence hangs her head. "As you command, your Majesty."

I shut off the link to Prudence and pull up Hunter on the monitor wall.

"What's up, Caelin?" he asks.

"I need you to escort Prudence from the building. Now."

Hunter nods. "As you command."

The last thing I do is shut off all surveillance in the middle room. Not sure why I feel so strongly about this, but whatever happens with me and Lexa, I don't want it recorded.

And I go in.

35

LEXA

*A*fter stepping into the newly-opened entrance in the wall, I find myself in a darkened passageway. The scent of freshly-oiled wood hangs in the air. Between that smell and the darkness, an odd thought appears in my mind.

This is like being inside a coffin.

Which, as it turns out, is a bad thought that leads to worse ideas. Everyone's heard the rumors about Caelin. A shiver runs down my spine.

Could Caelin be a vampire with mind control powers?

The moment the question enters my head, I toss it out like yesterday's trash. I'm a practical girl who lives in the real world. Supernatural stuff belongs on a movie screen, nothing more.

My heels click along the wooden floor as I make my way through the shadows. At last, I reach the end of the hallway. The next door is closed, but its shape is outlined by the light beyond.

That's where Caelin awaits. My heart thuds faster.

I press my palm against the door. It swings open with barely any pressure. Stepping across the threshold, I enter a fancy version of Lucky Ladies. But, where Otto's place is all torn furniture covered in questionable stains, this room holds real leather club chairs. Across from the sitting area, there's also a large wooden desk. Red velvet curtains cover the windows. Plush oriental rugs line the floor. Oil paintings of the Scottish country-side cover the walls.

On a nearby couch sits the exact man I've seen in my halluci-nations. Turns out, my imagination is pretty accurate. Caelin's broad shoulders fill out his dark suit perfectly. Every strand of his dark hair is combed back, highlighting his intense stare.

Oh, those eyes.

Caelin is the kind of man who looks right through you. I feel exposed, like my soul is laid bare. Caelin also sports the perfect level of scruff on his chin, too. I'm a sucker for that.

I brace myself, waiting for the lights to flash. That doesn't happen. There's no mist either.

A weight seeps off my shoulders. This is the real Caelin and that's all. I'm meeting him for the first time. No hallucinations. A sense of pride swells my rib cage.

Whatever's behind these hallucinations, I can handle it.

And it's that newfound confidence that I blame for what happens next.

I set my fist on my hip and run off my mouth. "If you want to see my tits and ass, take me out to a nice dinner first. You know, like an actual man with real balls."

With that, it's official. I've left behind any scrap of Mom's *shut up and do what he says* plan.

Caelin watches me for a long minute. And I might be imag-ining things, but it seems that his lips are parted in an expression of disbelief.

I squint and get a better look. Turns out, I'm totally right. His mouth is hanging open.

Score one for Lexa.

Still, this is a powerful guy and I just insulted his balls. It may be time to vamoose. I start inching backward toward the exit.

And Caelin laughs his ass off.

"I'm glad you find this amusing." I turn, ready to speed away.

But the door is gone.

This is the same as what happened back in Prudence's office. Before, I couldn't see the door in the first place... then, it just opened. Now, the exit closes up so quietly, I didn't even realize it shut. Trouble is, I can't leave without asking for help. And did I just insult his balls?

Yes, I did.

Talk about awkward.

Caelin gestures to the opposite side of the couch. "Have a seat."

"You're not pissed off about the balls thing?"

A devious twinkle shines in his dark eyes. "Nae. And I didn't approve Prudence's odd request for you to strip. Although it's true that every inch of this building is tracked on camera. My lifestyle demands top-level security."

My heart lightens. *This is good.* Before, I worried Caelin was a nut job. But it seems he's just a rich man with strange tastes. We see this in Lucky Ladies all the time. Super-wealthy dudes come in. You'd think they'd want folks sucking up to them. They don't. Some guys love slumming it with people who insult their balls. Go figure.

I exhale a long breath. *Maybe this could work.*

"I haven't laughed that hard in a hundred years," adds Caelin.

"A *hundred* years?"

"Aye."

My soaring thoughts now take a major nosedive. *This guy is serious. A hundred years?* I scan the walls again, searching for that exit.

Caelin follows my gaze. Once more, I have that creepy feeling that he knows exactly what I'm thinking. And in this case? It's a quick departure.

"I mean that in a manner of speaking, of course," he adds.

"Cool. Great. Awesome."

Stop talking, Lexa.

Caelin gestures to the other side of the couch once more. "Please."

This time, I take him up on the offer. Only, I'm still not too sure about this guy, so I park my ass as far away as possible. Still, as sitting experiences go, this is one of my best. The red leather is literally smooth as butter. It's as if someone's massaging my ass.

A realization hits me. *This is go time.* Before I leave here, Caelin must commit to keeping me and my family safe from every enemy of Konstantin the Rus. And he must do it all while maintaining Sash's meds from Silver Pharma.

No pressure.

CAELIN

*L*exa sits as far away as possible while still technically taking a seat on my couch. So far, I've soaked in different aspects of this woman. I've met Fierce Lexa, Passionate Lexa, and Witty Lexa. This new version is something different. Worried Lexa.

Is it because she's been enhanced by the Gray Woman?

Up close, I notice how Lexa's boxy jacket covers her wrists. The main reason I need to meet Lexa is to find out if she's been enhanced by the Gray Woman. It's the best explanation for our ongoing hallucinations: the classic power of a mindlock daemon.

Before Lexa leaves this room, I will find out what the Gray Woman did to her.

"Time for formal introductions," I begin. "I'm Caelin MacGregor."

"I'm Alexa Uznetsov. Everyone calls me Lexa. I'm here about your personal assistant job." She tilts her head. "Prudence was a little sketchy on the job, other than taking off my clothes."

"My apologies for that," I state. "When Prudence asked you to strip, I almost burst into the room. You bested her before I could reach the door."

"Oh." She smiles. Our gazes lock. A line of connection forms between us. Energy pulses between our souls. I half-expect the lights to flicker or mist to roll in. Before anything can happen, Lexa clears her throat and looks away.

It's the second time she's done that. When I meet someone's gaze, few have the power to look away. It's yet another factor that supports that Lexa is enhanced.

"You've a strange accent," says Lexa. "It's Scottish and not."

"I may appear young, but I've seen much of the world. No one speaks like I do." I tilt my head. "What d'ye think I do all day?"

Lexa shrugs. "I don't know. Race around in sports cars? Toss cash out windows?"

I can't help but smile. "People come to me with ideas on how to make money. Sometimes I invest. Afterward, I must check how things work out. Do know anything about that?"

I bob my head, considering. "I know when people are bullshitting me. Does that count?"

"Aye, that it does. I need someone to help track investments. I'm a night person. You could be my counterpart during daylight hours."

"I could do that. Maybe. But, you're suspicious as hell."

"As are you." I lean forward, resting my elbows on my knees. "I'll do you the honor of being honest."

"Sure. Thanks, I guess."

"There are forces at work here beyond the human world. Supernaturals. Elementals. Vampires."

Lexa's eyes widen. "Huh."

She's getting nervous, but I'm not sure how much of it is an act. Surely, if she works for Konstantin, she must suspect that bloodkin exist.

"There's a water elemental who is parading around as a human," I continue. "It's Dr. Gray of Silver Pharmaceutical. She's trying to enhance humans with the capabilities of vampires, such as the ability to inspire fear, desire, or stealth. As in, vampires can use mind control to convince others we aren't in the room. Are you with me so far?"

Lexa nods.

"I have reason to believe you may have been injected with an enhancement from Silver Pharma. It's based on the powers of a mindlock daemon. And it gives you the ability to inspire hallucinations in others. My offer of employment is genuine, but it must be based on complete honesty between us. Tell me; when and how did you get enhanced?"

Lexa stands up and loses her mind.

"What the actual fuck are you talking about? There's no such thing as vampires. Who told you I've been having hallucinations?" She rolls her eyes. "Who am I kidding? Anyone at Paxton High would tell you that."

"We need to discuss reality here. Show me your wrists. I must see your injection mark. Silver Pharma needles leave an unmistakable trace on the skin. I'll know the enhancement by the pattern."

"What? No way."

I sense her pulse, lock onto it, and press magic into my voice. "SHOW ME YOUR WRISTS."

"I've had it here. I am done."

What cocktail of powers did the Gray Woman give Lexa? Hallucinations are odd, but nothing I can't handle. But the ability to push back on my mind control? I've never felt anything like it.

A darker option appears. Lexa is human. Perhaps being close to me is what's causing the problem, regardless of whatever the Gray Woman has done.

Red madness. I might be the one driving Lexa insane. I force myself to sit still as Lexa steps away.

I must let her go.

37

LEXA

Vampires?
    Elementals?

This is beyond belief.

Clearly, Caelin's too unhinged to help keep himself safe, let alone protect me and my family. I came here because I thought Caelin could help. Still, he's not the only possibility.

Despair is the last refuge of the unimaginative.

I'll figure something out, I always do.

Even better, I've proven to myself that I don't have hallucinations *around* Caelin MacGregor, only *about* Caelin MacGregor. Which means that any reason to be inside Empire Investments is over.

I'm done here.

I step up to the stretch of wall where I first entered the room. There's no sign of the secret door, but that's not a problem right now.

I've heard stories of grandmas who lift Mack trucks with enough adrenaline. That must be what's happening to me, because I punch the wall, tear open the door, and speed walk away from Caelin.

Once again, the exit passage feels like being trapped inside a coffin. *Whatever.* In no time, I'm walking out the second door and into Prudence's office.

The head of HR is gone.

Good news.

I yank on the exit door. That part goes well. What happens next is a shock. Someone blocks my exit.

It's Vice.

This is the same kid I knew from high school. Only now, Vice wears dark battle leathers with a fur cape hanging from his shoulders. A line of black paint cuts across his face, highlighting his already-large eyes.

A dagger with an obelisk-shaped blade is gripped in his fist.

At first, all I can do is stare in shock. That's all the invitation Vice needs. He lunges right for me.

I move away faster than I thought possible. Vice grasps the back of my white jacket. I unzip it and back off. Unfortunately, I retreat to a corner of the room with no exit.

Vice races for me. His blade seems to move in slow motion as it angles toward my heart.

At the last moment, the blade is stopped. Caelin now stands before me, his face angry as thunder. He twists Vice's arm until something snaps. At the same time, Caelin looks toward me.

"Run," he states.

I don't need to be told twice. I take off down the hallway. From the corner of my eye, I see another figure wearing a fur cape. Must be a member of Vice's gang.

I grab a nearby handle and push open a random door. Slipping inside, I find myself in a large meeting room with a long table and tall windows. No one's here.

It's as good a place to hide as any.

With silent movements, I shut the door, wait, and listen. A light footstep paces the hallway before marching away. Mechanical groans follow as the elevator doors open and close.

I exhale. Whoever it is, they're gone.

I reach for the handle once more, ready to slip away at last. My fingers are inches away when the door flies open. Once again, someone blocks my exit.

Before, it was Vice.

This time, it's Prudence.

Alarm rattles through my nervous system. For some reason, the Vice President of HR now wears battle leathers and a fur cape. As with Vice, a line of black paint crosses her face at eye level. She's also washed off her make-up, revealing blue tattoos along her face and neck. I suspected Prudence was unhinged, but nothing like this.

Throwing up my hands, I say the first thing that comes to mind.

"What is wrong with you people?"

38

CAELIN

*a*sking Lexa about vampires and elementals? Not my best idea.
In my defense, I assumed we'd discuss the Gray Woman. Instead, Lexa stormed from the room... but only after tearing open the hidden door to reception.

This isn't the first time a human has done this, by the way. I chalk it up to the magic of adrenaline.

Still, Lexa is my guest. I want to ensure she leaves safely. All of which is why I now follow her at what I hope is a discrete distance. As it turns out, I misjudged the situation again.

By the time I reach the reception room, Lexa is no longer alone. There are a handful of employees who work at this level of the building. None of them stroll about in Rus warrior garb.

I've no doubt that Hunter already escorted my Vice Present of Human Resources to the exit. Somehow, Prudence's brother, Vice, got into the building and is about to spear Lexa with an obelisk blade.

White-hot rage courses through my body. *Lexa is here under my protection—how dare this human try to hurt her?* I move with supernatural speed and block Vice's strike.

I speak one word to Lexa. "Run."

While Lexa speeds away, I round on Vice. "We need to talk. I'll give you one chance to do so willingly."

Vice laughs.

Guess that means his answer is *no.*

I tap into the pulse of Vice's heart. Once I have the rhythm in my mind, I speak my next command with vampire power. "Why are you here?"

"You think you're the hero," says Vice. "You're a villain. Fyodor the Rus was a great king. Konstantin should have followed his father and protected him. Instead, your so-called friend allowed Fyodor to be killed. Later, Konstantin stood by while you married his sister. I'm here to end you. And Konstantin is next."

"I've been following Konstantin's little earner for weeks," adds Vice. "I even dropped off the postcard that lured her here. Once I'm done with you, I'll make sure she's next. And I'll kill Konstantin last."

"Where did you hear of Fyodor the Rus? Was it from the nightling at the Cloisters?"

His face reddens while he speaks through gritted teeth. "Don't have… to answer."

"I disagree." Tapping into my inner energy, I press even more vampire magic into my voice. "WHERE?"

"My enhancements… fully active… block you." Vice shivers. It isn't easy for him to press back on my mind control, yet he's still doing it.

What kind of enhancement delivers that ability?

Reaching forward, I grab Vice's hand. Indeed, there is a mark on his wrist. Only it's not the looping eternity symbol I've seen so many times before. Instead, it's the letter K in looping script.

If the infinity symbol means vampire power, then what does a K mean?

I open my mouth, ready to ask Vice that exact question. There isn't time to speak a word.

Vice crumples over in pain as his body transforms. While his overall height and muscle mass balloon, Vice's arms elongate until they're covered in snake scales and green slime. The skin on his face shrinks back, leaving his eyes as dual points of green flame. Great protective spikes erupt from his chest and legs.

I no longer need to ask Vice what kind of injection the Gray Woman gave him. The man has the powers of a killflare daemon, a fire elemental who loves nothing more than to destroy. The green slime on his arms is highly toxic, even to vampires. It won't kill bloodkin, but it does slow us down. And those spikes on Vice's chest are more than protective. He can snap any of them off to use as a stake.

What is the Gray Woman up to? Why even create a creature like this? It's no secret that she has a chaotic nature. Still, there's wanting to disrupt the world... and there's creating a humanoid killflare.

I set the thought aside. There will be time to deal with the Gray Woman later. For now, I need to face my opponent.

Killflare Vice reaches toward my hand. A moment ago, I grabbed Vice's wrist. Now, I dodge his touch. Vice's scaly arm slams into the floor with enough force to break through the wooden slats.

Little by little, Killflare Vice rises to his full height. He now looms a good three feet taller than I am. I remove my obelisk blade from under my jacket. Fire daemons are tricky to destroy. I scan the office and quickly come up with a plan.

Killflare Vice comes at me while pinwheeling his arms. Green goop flies off in every direction. Each time his scaly appendage slams into the floor, it breaks through the wood planks and steel bars beneath.

I grasp the top of Prudence's desk and flip it vertical to use it as a shield. Once Killflare Vice is close enough, I slam the desk's bottom into my opponent's body, shoving him across the room.

All the while, Killflare Vice pushes against me, his poisonous arms flailing.

It's a tug of war as my opponent fights me while I shove him toward a particular spot by the wall. Once I have Killflare Vice pinned, I toss my obelisk dagger toward the ceiling.

Snap!

My blade hits the sprinkler valve right above Killflare Vice's head. The device comes to life, raining water onto my enemy. Killflare Vice screeches and convulses. Using Prudence's desk, I hold my enemy in place until he's not only motionless on the floor, but the green fire in his eyes is gone.

Vice is dead.

Tossing the desk aside, I stare at the broken and monstrous body before me. *Such a waste of life.* If there's one bright spot, I can console myself knowing that I ended Vice in time. Not that I worry about Konstantin fighting a humanoid killflare. But there was another target on Vice's list.

If nothing else, Lexa is safe.

39

LEXA

*T*his just keeps getting weirder and weirder. Today is like Alice in Wonderland, only my version of the story includes vampires and insane HR chicks.

Prudence stalks into the meeting room. I'd tell her to step aside, but she holds some kind of strange dagger. As Prudence moves forward, I step back.

"You should have left," says Prudence. "There's no reason for me to make you strip. I wanted you to run." Raising the dagger higher, she angles the weapon at my heart.

"I could still run." I take a side-step. She matches the movement. "Or not."

"I wanted to kill you later, not now. If you'd been just a little bit patient, I could have used my new gifts."

I think back to my last hallucination. In it, I saw Prudence begging some lady in a lab coat for an enhancement. Maybe my crazy is aligning with her crazy.

All the more reason to flee.

When I next speak, I take care to use my most calming tone. "How nice for you. But I have an idea. Maybe it's better not to kill me."

"No, if I don't kill you, my brother Vice will. He's been following you, studying your every move. You're not leaving here alive."

Prudence accents this last point by widening her eyes. It's an especially creepy stare, considering how she's now got a band of black goop across her face.

My thoughts spin. I'm a surveillance girl by nature. I like having time to come up with the right approach. Perhaps it's the adrenaline rush, but a plan suddenly appears.

Maybe my crazy can REALLY align with her crazy.

I make jazz hands. I'm not proud of this fact, but I want to live. "I've got magic."

"You're lying."

"You know who thinks I've got magic going on? Caelin. I'm an, um, elemental vampire daemon enhancer."

Not my best.

Quick as a whip, she grabs my hand and scans the skin along my wrist. "You're not enhanced."

I pull my hand out of her grasp. "Back off or I'll use my mojo on you."

"You're not enhanced. I know who you are. I saw you and your sister climb Siniy Mountain to see the Gray Woman, just as my I did with my brother. You asked Zhenshchina Vody for mercy and she froze you into a tomb of ice. I saw you writhing on the floor, fighting back her seaweed tentacles. You're nothing but a powerless human."

Every cell in my body vibrates with rage. Sometimes, Sash will mention vampires and I lose my temper. That's nothing compared to the level of pure fury that runs through me at this moment.

"In memory of Fyodor the Rus, I shall kill the favorite of his useless son, Konstantin." She grips the dagger so tightly, her knuckles flare white. "This is Fyodor's old blade. I stole it from Caelin. Now, I'll use it to kill you."

Power rises inside me. Energies align. Fury takes over. "My life is done already," I counter. "All I do is worry about my sister and hold never-ending stakeouts for Konstantin. Then, I get these weird hallucinations with none other than Caelin MacGregor. And this here? It's probably another fake vision to add into the bunch. Well, I've had it!"

Prudence lunges for me. Something inside me snaps. While holding my ground, I yell my lungs out.

"If you want to stab someone, stab yourself! Did you hear me? STAB YOURSELF!"

Prudence stops in place. Her face falls slack.

I march out of the room, slamming the door behind me.

Bitch.

40

CAELIN

*V*ice lays on the floor, immobile. I'm about to check his pulse when his body begins convulsing. His size collapses. Spikes retract into his chest and legs. Even Vice's head and arms return to normal.

Kneeling down, I set my fingertips on his neck. There's no pulse.

Anger rises within me. The Gray Woman turned this human into an ancient warrior bent on my destruction. Not sure how Fyodor the Rus got into the mix, but I'm sure it made sense in the Gray Woman's mind.

Hunter bursts into the room. "I showed her out, but she snuck back in."

It's an effort to snap my thoughts out of Vice and the Gray Woman. "Who?"

"Prudence," explains Hunter. "She made copies of all your skeleton keys. Some of the employees saw her sneaking around in body armor and a fur cape."

Shock careens through my nervous system. "Lexa."

I rush out into the hallway while calling out to Hunter. "Make sure the building is cleared." Hunter rushes off in the opposite direction.

I'm not halfway down the passage when the smell of blood turns overwhelming. Following the scent, I speed off toward a particular meeting room. There's no heartbeat here, only the coppery tang of death.

Please, let Lexa be okay.

I whip open the door to find an unexpected scene. Prudence lies on the floor. Just as Hunter reported, Prudence wears battle leathers and a fur cape. Her face is marked with the classic signs of a Rus warrior.

And she's dead.

Prudence clutches the handle of an obelisk dagger. She plunged the weapon into her own heart. Even from a distance, I can tell what blade she used. *Fyodor's dagger.*

The way Prudence holds the weapon, I can clearly see her wrists. Like Vice, there's a stylized scar on her skin. This time, the mark reads SP, probably for Silver Pharma. Only unlike her brother, Prudence's marks are freshly scarred over.

It's clear what happened. After years of pleading, Prudence convinced the Gray Woman to inject her with enhancements. Only these injections aren't for the proven vampire skills. The Gray Woman gave Prudence new and unproven DNA from primal daemons.

And it drove Prudence mad. The woman stabbed her own heart.

Another scent strikes me. Lexa was here. Did she see Prudence?

One way to find out.

I can access any security feed from my cell. Taking out my phone, I sort through recent footage. There's some video of Prudence marching into the network center of Empire Investments. To get in, she used my skeleton keys, just as Hunter reported.

After that, all the building feeds go dead. Prudence cut them off to hide what she was about to do. And if her goal was the same as Vice's, then she wanted to kill me in revenge for Fyodor's death.

Vice and Prudence must have connected with the rogue nightlings from the Cloisters. It's the only way to explain how they both became obsessed with Fyodor.

Yet, no matter how this happened, there's one person who knows the truth. The Gray Woman. First thing tomorrow morning, I'll return to Silver Pharma. It's time Dr. Gray stopped speaking in riddles.

I take in one last breath, happy to catch a final wisp of Lexa's scent. When she's near, I reconnect to the man I once was. King Caelin. This room. This moment. It's all I'll have of that sensation.

Iona was right all those years ago. It's my curse to destroy the women I care about, especially the humans. Sadly, Prudence was the closest thing I had to a regular female presence.

I scan Prudence's broken body and ancient costume. A weight of sorrow settles into my bones. In our own way, we relied on each other.

And this is how her life ends.

I won't let it happen to Lexa.

41

LEXA

*M*y Empire Investments interview is the definition of the word, *disaster*. After leaving the building, I splurge on a cab to Lucky Ladies. During the ride back, I dissect everything that happened.

First, there's Caelin. Things went pretty well there... until the infamous chat about vampires and elementals.

Second comes the HR minion, Prudence. She starts off by asking me to strip. Later on, she goes into evil cosplay mode, dressing up like a furry gladiator and trying to skewer me, shish kebab style.

Third, some good stuff happens. I walk out of the building like a boss. And I didn't have one hallucination.

By rights, I should be freaking out. Normally, I live in the shadows. Today, I hit the spotlight for an interview with an odd CEO along and a loco HR lady. By this point, I should be huddled in the corner of this cab, rocking in terror.

I'm not.

If anything, I feel ten feet tall and ready to climb a mountain. Or more specifically, to march right into the Lucky Ladies without even thinking my classic mantra.

Because today, I'm visible.

I head back to my bedroom, crack out my drawing pad, and get to work. The world vanishes while it's only my pencils and ideas. When I'm finished, I have an image of me in a red dress. As in, the crimson gown Cartier picked out for me. And in the image, I hold a violin.

Clearly, part of me wants to hit the House of Music tonight.

What a great idea.

I check my satchel. Sure enough, I still have the postcards about the House of Music. I tap the cards against my palm. An idea forms.

I always carry the burden of Sash's illness, Konstantin's heists, and Mom's uselessness. Maybe for one night, I set it all aside. I'll be beautiful and strong... Someone who can do anything.

Otto pounds his fist on the closed door to my room. "Where's my report? I'm supposed to get it today."

I reset the notebook under my bed. "I'm not giving you anything."

Otto slides aside the plank of wood that serves as my door. He stands framed on the threshold. The man's never looked more sweaty, bald, and round. His tiny eyes are alight with rage.

"What did you say?"

"I'm not finishing the report," I reply casually.

I smile, thinking through Sash's words. *You deliver enough to Konstantin. You can rattle his cage once in a while.*

Cage, consider yourself rattled.

"I'm calling Konstantin," says Otto.

"Aren't you going to ask me *why* first?"

"Don't fuck with me."

"Today, Vice dressed up like a barbarian and got stabbed by none other than Caelin MacGregor. I just happened to notice the dead body as I was running to catch the elevator. Long story."

"You *are* fucking with me."

"That story is too weird not to be true. Call Konstantin."

"You better not be lying to me, Lexa." Otto storms from the room. I let out a contented sigh.

For what should be a disaster of a day, I'm certainly having a good time. And that postcard from the House of Music is still clasped in my hands.

Is this really happening?

I sashay to the performer's dressing room and check the rolling garment racks. Sure enough, my dress is still there. I step over to Cartier's prep station. All her makeup is laid out, along with a little note saying, *You better use this, Lexa.*

I smile so hard, my face hurts. *Oh, this is happening.*

42

CAELIN

Cleaning up after Prudence and Vice isn't easy. Disposing of the bodies is the easy part. What's tougher is finding who might have seen the two of them dressed up as Rus warriors. I can block someone from detecting my presence. Once the memory is formed, it's a lot harder to wipe out.

For this reason, I only employ bloodkin, nightling, or humans who know that vampires exist. Even so, the occasional outsider can get into the building. Fortunately, few people saw Prudence and Vice in their new attire. The ones that did can be trusted to keep the secret.

After clean-up is done, I head back to my penthouse and soak in my favorite view of the city. It's a clear night, so moonlight dances across the water. The ferry boats leave long and elegant wakes behind them. It's calm, but none of that peace enters my heart.

How I miss Elisava.

I head into my private library. Ebony bookshelves line the walls. An old Persian carpet covers the floor. A few black leather chairs surround the fireplace. I step over to a particular stretch of shelves and tip down one of the novels. A panel of bookshelves swings open, revealing a small alcove behind it.

This is a special place I built. Candles flare to life once the alcove is opened. The walls are a mosaic of gray stones, all of which were taken from the beach outside my old castle. In the center of the small space, there's a tall platform that holds a bust of Elisava. The artist who created this is so talented, it seems as if my wife could come alive and speak.

I brush the back of my fingertips down Elisava's cold cheek. "Remember the day we wed? My father had just passed. I was the new king. My people knew me as a good man who was far more interested in women and battle than anything else. When we decided to marry, my nobles complained. But who should come marching down the beach? The Gray Woman."

I imagine what Elisava would say if she were here now. It would be something about the Gray Woman's kindness, no doubt. Elisava always thought the best of everyone.

"The Gray Woman announced that she'd looked into the waters of time," I continue. "In every possible future, I would become a great king. But by marrying you, I'd also keep my good heart. None of my nobles wanted the clan to treat humans, bloodkin, and nightling equally. Without you, I wouldn't have had the strength to do it."

I soak in her wide eyes and gentle smile. Elisava would always calm me with the barest look.

Bring me some of that tranquility now, Elisava. I need it.

"Years have passed," I state. "Little by little, my heart has been worn away. Only a sliver remains, and that remnant burns with grief whenever I think of you."

I close the door, resetting it so no one would tell anything was hidden behind this wall of books.

Suddenly, the lights flare. Mist rolls in. I'm encased in a white cloud. The haze is so thick, I can barely see my hand before my face. When the haze fades, I'm no longer in my apartment.

I stand in a grand ballroom with a domed ceiling. Partygoers in fancy dress step around the room. A chamber orchestra launches into Pachabel's Canon. A placard on their stage reads House of Music.

Lexa saunters into the room. She looks stunning in a red dress. As she smiles, my dead heart flares to life. A voice sounds from nowhere.

She is yours.

That speaker sounds a lot like Elisava.

Lights flicker once more. Mist rolls in again. The next thing I know, I'm back in my apartment.

And I know what to do.

LEXA

*H*ouse of Music started off as a vaudeville music hall before becoming a movie house and, most recently, a place for live music, fancy dress, and cocktails.

I'm going there tonight.

Can't wait.

To reach the House of Music, I splurge on another cab ride. It's just past nine o'clock when I step onto the curb before the building itself. Moonlight reflects off the sidewalk, making the concrete glisten like diamonds. Before me stands a three-story building with green facade that's carved with great arches. A golden marquee covers the entrance. Above it, House of Music is written in swirly black letters.

Men in tuxedos and ladies in formal gowns step through the entrance. As I follow them inside, I catch my own reflection in the glass doors. My brown hair hangs in loose curls over my shoulders. The red dress fits my curves just right. And I even found a little red clutch to match.

I saunter through the entry hall and into the ballroom. It's got an arched ceiling covered with murals of ladies from the 1800's. All of them wear long gowns like mine. Lines of filigree and flowers entwine all the images together, cascading down the walls and onto the mosaic floor.

A waist-high platform covers the far wall of the room. The show's already begun, as shown by how the green curtain's already parted. The violin couple from Big Apple Coffee play onstage with a small orchestra. They finish up a tune as I approach.

The pair see me, smile, and whisper among the other musicians. The mini-orchestra then launches into *Pachabel's Canon*.

An electric twinge crawls up my back. *Someone's looking at me.* I step around in a slow circle. A few people glance my way. Their gazes are casual and respectful. In other words, it's nothing like what happens with Otto's infamous bikini contests.

No one's seriously staring in my direction. I shrug. *Maybe I'm imagining things.*

I step up to the bar and wait for the bartender to come around. Not that I'm in any rush. While I wait, I pay close attention to everyone else's orders. I've been in a bar before, but it's easy to ask for *'whatever beer is on tap.'* Ordering fancy drinks is something else.

Turns out, all the names are way too long to remember. And I'm not sure if I'll like any of them. When the bartender gets to me, he has an open face with big blue eyes and a goatee.

"What would you like?" he asks.

"Wine?"

"Red or white?"

"How about you surprise me?" I cup my hand by my mouth and lower my voice. "I'm new at this."

The bartender leans back and scans me carefully. "I think…" He screws up his mouth to one side of his face. "You're a pinot noir girl." He pours me a glass of red wine. I take a dainty sip.

The bartender arches his right eyebrow. "What do you think?"

"Delicious. It takes like dark grapes, if that makes sense."

"It does."

I pay in cash and make sure to leave a big tip. At the same time, the orchestra strikes up a tango. A group of partygoers race out to the dance floor. Small round tables are set at the room's periphery. I grab an empty seat, sip my wine, and watch couples dance.

As the minutes pass, a strange desire rises within my mind. Some twisted part of me wishes the lights would flash, announcing that my dream Caelin will stop by for a visit. After all, I look about as good as possible right now. It would be beyond lovely to have Caelin peel off this dress.

I sigh and take another sip. Caelin or not, I definitely need more moments like this one. And if I can't live it through an hallucination?

Then, I'll always have my imagination.

CAELIN

*L*ess than an hour later, I step through the front doors to the House of Music. It's a classic art nouveau building with lots of lavish murals, faux jade, and swirling lines. I straighten the lapel of my tuxedo and step into the ballroom.

There's no sign of Lexa.

Hands down, this is one of the most unhinged things I've ever done. Chances are, Lexa is enhanced to give me hallucinations. Face to face was one thing. Now, I'm getting long-distance messages.

I step around the edge of the room. Music swells. Couples tango on the dance floor. The lights dim.

Still no Lexa.

I've given this enough time. Come tomorrow morning, I can return to Silver Pharma and press the Gray Woman for answers. Lexa probably doesn't understand what injections she received anyway.

An image appears in my mind. It's the primal daemon version of Vice, complete with a skull-like face and tentacle arms. Who'd ask for that? I doubt Vice knew what he was getting into, either.

I head for the exit. That's when I see her.

Lexa leans against a nearby stretch of wall. My breath catches. She's nothing less than a goddess in her red gown. Life and drive still gleam in her eyes. The woman's like a magnet, drawing me closer.

I take one step nearer.

Two.

A question appears. Am I doing this for the right reasons? I've failed to protect my blood sisters, fellow warriors, and even Elisava. Is there any reason to think I won't destroy Lexa? Sure, she's lovely and strong now. But with me nearby, her light will go out and leave only pain behind.

I must leave.

The decision weighs on me like so many stones. Most days, I only feel as if I've retained thin sliver of a heart. Now, even that feeling dies in my soul.

Nothing else to be done.

I turn away.

As I march toward the exit archway, I catch a flare of light in my peripheral vision. My skin chills over with stock. Turning, I see the new source of brightness.

It's Lexa. A crimson mark glows on her neck.

This can't be happening.

Yet, it is. A new tattoo marks her throat—a cluster of fiery tendrils. And it sparks as if created by red flame. *Magic.* I scan the faces nearby. None of them notice the bright symbol.

Everything that happened churns through my mind. From the first sight of Lexa, her inner strength and passion inspired me. She could rebuke my mind control without effort. And her resistance to the idea of vampires speaks to an inner and hidden knowledge.

Suddenly, Prudence's death takes on a new meaning. Lexa must have ordered Prudence to kill herself.

I think back to my last conversation with the Gray Woman.

We were standing before dozens of massive ice blocks. Each one contained a frozen person.

You aren't asking the right question.

Looking back, it's now clear why the Gray Woman showed me the blocks of ice. The first time I saw the cold storage room was in Silver Pharma. It seemed logical that all the frozen bodies were only as old as the building.

I was wrong.

The Gray Woman must have been putting test subjects on ice for a thousand years, probably longer. Which means Prudence and Vice weren't told about Fyodor the Rus. They knew the man. The Gray Woman froze them in ancient times, bringing them back for the modern era.

Joy and shock battle it out in my nervous system. I've been so blinded by my grief over Elisava, I haven't seen the truth before me. The Gray Woman kept her word. She saved the female bloodkin, or at least one of them.

Lexa lives. She's my fated mate.

The marks on Lexa's neck are unmistakable. No one else can see them because they aren't meant to—that fire is for me alone. And our hallucinations aren't from injections. Those visions are the natural result of growing cords of love and life.

Our unique magic.

It's so wondrous and beautiful, I want to capture this moment and relive it forever. Because for the first time in ages, hope sparks in my heart.

Lexa changes everything.

∿

The story continues in book 2, VEILS AND VAMPIRES!

ALSO BY CHRISTINA BAUER

VEILS AND VAMPIRES

BOOK 2, VAMPIRES OF THE DAEMONVERSE

The adventure and romance continues in VEILS AND VAMPIRES!

ANGELBOUND

Check out ANGELBOUND, the paranormal romance under my pen name, Christina Bauer!

FAIRY TALES OF THE MAGICORUM

Love fairy tales? Check out WOLVES AND ROSES!

DIMENSION DRIFT

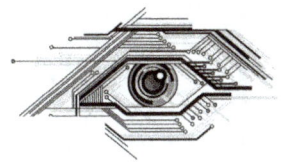

Want a strong sci-fi heroine and story? Read SCYTHE!!!

BEHOLDER

Like GAME OF THRONES? You'll love the BEHOLDER series!

STANDARD APPENDIX OF COOL STUFF

C

IF YOU ENJOYED THIS BOOK...

...Please consider leaving a review, even if it's just a line or two. Every bit truly helps, especially for those of us who don't *write by the numbers,* if you know what I mean.

Plus I have it on good authority that every time you review an indie author, somewhere a bloodkin finds their fated mate. For reals.

And angels need their caffeine, too.

COLLECTED WORKS

Vampires of the Daemonverse

Adult vampire romance

1. Violins and Vampires
2. Veils and Vampires
3. Vixens and Vampires
4. Valor and Vampires

Angelbound Series (paranormal romance)

Origins

1. Angelbound
2. Scala
3. Acca
4. Thrax
5. The Dark Lands
6. The Brutal Time
7. Armageddon
8. Quasi Redux
9. Clockwork Igni
10. Lady Reaper
11. Angry Gods

12. Phantom Corsair

Fairy Tales of the Magicorum (Fairy Tale Retellings)

Dimension Drift (science fiction)

1. Scythe, 2. Umbra, 3. Alien Minds, 4. ECHO Academy.
Finished series.

Pixieland Diaries (paranormal romance)

1. Pixieland Diaries, 2. Calla, 3. Dare.
Finished series.

Beholder (epic fantasy)

1. Cursed, 2. Concealed, 3. Cherished, 4. Crowned, 5. Cradled.
Finished series.

ACKNOWLEDGMENTS

If you're reading my freaking acknowledgements, chances are, I should thank you for something. So, for the record: you are awesome, dear reader.

That said, huge and heartfelt thanks must go out to my husband and son for their rock-solid support. Being an author means a lot of early mornings, late nights, long weekends, and never-ending patience. You two are the best guys in the universe, period.

After that, I must thank the extensive network of reviewers, friends and colleagues who helped me build my writing chops in general. Gracias.

Finally, deep affection goes out to my late, much loved, and dearly missed Aunt Sandy and Uncle Henry. You saw the writer in me, always. Thank you, first and last.

ABOUT CEE BEE

CEE BEE lives in New England with her husband, son, and semi-insane golden retriever. Miss BEE writes stories that blend epic fantasy, toe-curling romance, and lots of sass. If you want immersive tales that transport you to fresh worlds (and new book boyfriends) then you've come to the right author. To learn more about CEE BEE, please visit www.ceebeeauthor.com.

CEE BEE also writes young adult fiction under the name Christina Bauer. These titles deliver the same epic fantasy goodness with a little less steam. Check out Christina Bauer's books at www.christinabauerauthor.com. There is a literal sh*t ton of them.

Stalk CEE BEE/Christina on Social Media

Website:
www.ceebeeauthor.com

Blog:
http://monsterhousebooks.com/blog/category/christina

Facebook:
https://www.facebook.com/authorBauer/

Instagram:
https://www.instagram.com/christina_cb_bauer/

Twitter:
@CB_Bauer

VLOG:
https://tinyurl.com/Vlogbauer

AUTHOR Q&A

*H*ope you enjoyed this book! Here are some questions and answers to give you an inside view of the story...

How does this story differ from the Kindle Vella version?

Kindle Vella is a platform for serialized fiction. Stories are told in episodes—roughly equal to chapters in the book world—and get released daily or weekly. It's a different style than a traditional novel or novella. To make this story work as a book, I ended up moving a bunch of content from future episodes into this release. Hope it works... And thanks to everyone who kicked my ass on pre-street version!

You mention a Russian fairy tale in the story called Sister Alionushka and Brother Ivanushka. Is that a real thing?

What a great question, Person Who Is Definitely Not Me! Sister Alionushka and Brother Ivanushka is an actual Russian fairy tale. It's a bit like Hansel and Gretel, only there are goats and magical bodies of water involved.

Are you related to the author Christina Bauer?

We are the same person. I write young adult fiction as

Christina Bauer. CEE BEE books are for adults who like more steam in their stories. http://www.ceebeeauthor.com

How will Konstantin handle any future relationship between Caelin and Lexa?

Two words: Not well.

What was the hardest part of this story to write?

All opening chapters kick my ass, but the one for this book KICKED MY ASS. I set the scene in a courtroom, on a camping trip, and even during a Rus raid. None of it worked. And the pain in the butt part is that for each opening I'd think, *I nailed it this time!* Then, I'd come back the next day and think, *fuuuuuuuck. This isn't ready yet.* I cheered after I came up with the naked mud wrestling opening.

Why use curse words?

Some of these characters are not nice people. It just didn't feel authentic for them to say *dang* or *fudge*.

If you also write as CEE BEE, how is this novel different from your other work as Christina Bauer?

My Christina Bauer books are all young adult. They follow a three-act structure as outlined in a book called *Save the Cat* by Blake Snyder. There's a lot more action and battle stuff in this approach. My CEE BEE style is closer to a traditional romance novel with a slow burn that ends with one big battle scene. While I was writing the book, I found that big fight scenes were stealing the spotlight from the spicier romance scenes.

How do you come up with this stuff?

Before I start a book, I know the key beats I want to hit. But, how I get there? That's a lot of trial and error. For instance, take the opening scene for this book. The first options didn't really give Caelin a chance to shine as a character. The final scene— a.k.a. having him happily fight in mud—showed Caelin's full character.

This story includes a unique period from a thousand years ago. How important was historical accuracy in your process?

I value historical accuracy a lot considering how much I changed it to make a different bloodkin version. All in all, I created a ton of backstory for this world. For instance, Lexa grew up in a palace with onion domes... which weren't invented until 1500's. This architecture plays into her backstory and I could have done three pages about it.

In the end, it all got boiled down to a line about seeing an onion dome burn. By the way, this is one of the hardest things about worldbuilding. I have to put it in the page and then delete it. Somehow, readers know it exists, even if it's not on the page.

Long story short, if you find something odd from a historical context, feel free to email me at cbauer@monsterhousebook s.com. I would love to rattle on about the very detailed explanations (that didn't make it to the book because it just stopped the flow).

I liked your book, what's the best thing I can do to help you?

If you do want to support my work, please write a review. That's the real big thing because it drives sales. Also super helpful are shout-outs on social media. Also-also, I love hearing from readers. You make my day! My contact details are listed below...

Stalk CEE BEE on Social Media

Website:
www.ceebeeauthor.com

Blog:
https://monsterhousebooks.com/blog/category/ceebee

Facebook:
https://www.facebook.com/CEEBEEauthor

Instagram:

https://www.instagram.com/christina_cb_bauer/

Twitter:
https://twitter.com/ceebeeauthor

BONUS CHAPTER

On the following pages, I've included a scene between Kostantin and Caelin in one of their clubs for the middle section (when Lexa is in high school) After I wrote it, I realized that it wasn't adding any new insights, so I cut it to keep the story moving.

Hope you enjoy it!

CAELIN

Twenty minutes later, I stand before another skyscrapers in Midtown. Sunbeams cast patterns across the concrete tower. On street level, a small sign reads Club Castle. Humans pace the sidewalks. Most wear suits. All are oblivious to the fact that I'm a vampire.

I pass through the revolving door and into the lobby. It's a wide space made of black marble. A guard sits behind a tall steel desk. He nods as I approach. It's Pavel, one of Konstantin's bloodkin from the old days. He's got a flat face with large blue eyes and a receding chin. It gives him the look of being constantly shocked.

"Inspecting Konstantin's latest investment?" asks Pavel.

I chuckle. "We both know that the money comes from me."

"At heart, Konstantin is a raider."

"And what might I be?"

"A penny pinching skinflint Scotsman."

I all-out laugh. "And proud of it."

"Hey, are you going to Legacy Night?" asks Pavel. "Konstantin is making everyone show."

"Nae." Winking, I pull on the handle and enter the club.

Although it's dark inside, there's no missing how the interior is an open space made of gray rock. The place is meant to look as if you're inside a castle.

Memories appear. I'm back in my old home with Elisava. A stone staircase winds around the walls, corkscrew style. I picture myself slogging up those steps with Elisva's body in my arms. An invisible wound opens in my chest, like my heart's been torn out.

Elisava is gone.

My bairn is no more.

Shaking my head, I force myself to return to the present moment. I stand in an open space that's four stories high. The spiral staircase is a modified set of balconies so partygoers can look out on the club floor. On the ground level, there's a stone-style bar backed by a wall of liquor. A central dance floor sits on the opposite side of the room. In the far corner, there's a hidden doorway that leads to a private club room.

I picture humans at the bar, on the dance floor, and watching the action from the many balconies connecting the stairs.

A door opens at the top balcony, casting a beam of light across the chamber. Konstantin steps out from his private office and pins me with an intense stare. The man looks the same as when I first met him a thousand years ago, including his bulky body, shaved head, tattoos and leathers. The only difference with this modern version is that he no longer paints a line of charcoal over his eyes.

Konstantin down to me. "Glad you're here. I was about to take this interrogation to the next level." He steps back inside his office.

A short climb later, I step inside one of Konstantin's many lairs. They all have the same basic set up. There's a massive desk with a throne-like chair and that's it. The message is clear—do your business and leave. The only thing Konstantin changes between lairs is the design. This one has the same stone look as the rest of the club.

A human cowers in the corner. He's a middle-aged human with a hefty build and shaved head. A logo for Lady Liberty Company is plastered across his shirt—that's one of the companies that transfers cargo on the New York harbor. The bruises on his face and neck says that this guy's been talking to Konstantin for some time.

"This is Bruce." When the Konstantin next speaks, his voice takes on the faint echo that means he's using the bloodkin power of mind control. "Tell him what you told me."

"No."

Konstantin's voice echoes even more deeply. "Tell him."

"I got enhanced," answers Bruce.

Konstantin and I share a long look. This is nothing new. The Gray Woman has been enhancing humans this way for years. We track the test subjects down. Either they join Empire Investments… or Konstantin makes them vanish.

"There's more," states Konstantin. "Talk. What else has she got you into?"

"Fuck you," says the human.

"Let me try." I press vampire power into my voice. "What else are you holding back on us"

"Your capos are lying to you. Mikhail stole three shipments for himself. And that's just the beginning."

"What else?"

"Grigory and Mila are taking even more," says Bruce.

"Anything else?" I ask. The human shakes his head. I press in more magic than ever before. "What else aren't you telling us?"

"Nothing."

I shake a look with my fellow bloodkin. Konstantin shakes his head. We don't need to say anything else. Both of us know this human has shared everything he knows.

"It's over," states Konstantin.

The human shivers. "Are you going to drink my blood?"

"No," says Konstantin. "You're tainted."

The human exhales. Konstantin steps forward, sets his hands on either side of the human's head, and twists. After his neck snaps and the human falls over, dead.

There was a time I'd mourn this loss of life. A thousand years ago, I'd have blocked Konstantin from even touching the human. At that time, it was important to me bloodkin, humans, and nightling coexisted. All that died with Elisava.

"How did the Gray Woman recruit this one?" I ask.

"He used to do maintenance in Central Park," answers Konstantin. "She appeared to him in a fountain."

"This human had coworkers and a family. There will be clean-up. You know the rules."

When it comes to Konstantin and death, my only requirement is that if he kills a human, he needs to clean up his messes. I don't want our kind exposed. Humans are growing more powerful with technology. Thanks to the bloodkin plague, there are also way too many of them.

"I always clean up my messes." Konstantin crosses his arms over his chest. That means he's scheming.

"What's going on in that twisted mind of yours?"

"Why should we be on the outside, trying to figure out what the Gray Woman is up to? Clearly, she's trying to recruit humans and only finding a bunch of zeros. We should team with the Gray Woman. Offer to help her find good humans."

"Nae. The Gray Woman is chaos incarnate. Whatever she's planning, it won't end well."

"We can't stop her, Caelin. The Gray Woman will keep recruiting humans." Konstantin gestures toward the dead human. "Right now, she's doing a piss poor job of it. You and I could do much better."

"*You* could," I declare. "I want no part of it."

"Think about it. If we help her with these enhancements, don't you think she could bring back the female bloodkin?"

"Never. All she'll do is cause more trouble, because that's all she is."

Konstantin shrugs. "Fine. I'll approach her alone."

"And don't ask me to fund this endeavor, either."

"Now, that's just rude. Some men are meant to spend money, others to save it. We're just two sides of the same coin."

I could debate Konstantin on this, but why bother? We're had this argument many times before. Konstantin lives for the thrill of the heist. And there's no rush if he has a full bank account.

Sometimes, I wish I'd never made that vow to Elisava.

"Shut up," says Konstantin.

"Shut up? I'm not saying anything."

"You don't need to." He taps my temple. "You're in my head. Just know this. I'll get my house in order. One day, I'll be richer than you, mark my words."

"In the meantime, what are you going to do with Grigory and Mila?"

"Why do you care?"

"You know why."

"Prudence's kid brother is living with those two." Konstantin groans. "Why should I care about Prudence? She's a liar."

"So are we. Prudence is useful."

Konstantin points at my nose. "You rely too much on that human."

"You only say that because Prudence won't work for you," I counter.

In fact, Prudence hates Konstantin. She says he killed someone she loved. Konstantin commits murder far too often for me to doubt her story. Still, Konstantin tried to recruit her, saying *money is thicker than blood.* I told Konstantin it was a fool's errand. My warning didn't stick, but that's Konstantin for you. Always out for the long shot. The rush.

"I'll check into the situation," says Konstantin. "If Grigory and Mila have stolen too much, they'll pay the price. This is business,

Caelin." He pauses. "Well, aren't you going to tell me to treat humans differently?"

"That was King Caelin's belief." I add in one final thought, just to clear up any confusion.

"King Caelin died a long time ago."

~